The Curse of Not Being Chosen

The Curse of Not Being Chosen

Vaibhav Singh Chandel

NU VOICE
PRESS

First published by NU VOICE PRESS 2026
An imprint of Hubhawks Pvt. Ltd
www.nuvoicepress.com

This is a work of fiction. Space and time have been rearranged to suit the convenience of the book. Except for public figures, hotels, and institution names, any resemblance to persons living or dead or the real events are purely coincidental. The opinions expressed in the book are those of the characters, and should not be confused with that of the Author.

ISBN: 978-81-995376-2-0
Typeset by Pooja Sharma
Published by Nu Voice Press

To Whom This Book Is Dedicated

This book is dedicated to all the people who have ever fallen in one-sided love.

One-sided love is a battle between hope and heartbreak.

Author's Note

Sometimes a story chooses the writer long before the writer chooses the story. *The Curse of Not Being Chosen* was born from the quiet ache that sits in all of us, the ache of loving deeply, silently, and without certainty.

This novel is not merely about heartbreak; it is about the weight of unspoken emotions, the courage it takes to love without being loved back, and the invisible battles people fight behind calm eyes and practiced smiles.

For anyone who has ever waited for a message that never came...

For anyone who stayed awake replaying conversations in the dark...

For anyone who loved quietly because speaking it aloud felt too dangerous...

this story is for you.

I wrote these chapters with trembling hands, because some pains are too tender to touch yet too powerful to ignore. If even one line makes you feel seen, understood, or a little less alone, then this story has done what it was born to do.

Thank you for letting these characters breathe in your heart.

Thank you for sharing this silence, this storm, and this journey with them.

With love,

Vaibhav Singh Chandel

The Curse of Not Being Chosen

"To my dearest love, you remain in my heart even though you were never mine. I cannot forget you, no matter how deeply I try to hide these feelings. Loving you in silence is both my greatest pain and my sweetest treasure."

Contents

Chapter 1
The Call That Changed Everything

Vijay Chandel's eyes moved swiftly across the files spread on the conference table. Around him, his team spoke in measured tones, presenting strategies and projections for a project that could redefine the company's future.

For most people, such meetings were exhausting, but for Vijay, they were his lifeblood. He had built his empire brick by brick, and every detail mattered. Rarely did anything pull him away from work.

Until that day.

A knock at the door broke the flow of discussion. Lisa, his trusted assistant, stepped in, her voice low.

"Sir… someone is here to see you."

Without looking up, Vijay replied, "Tell him I'm busy. Whatever it is can wait."

"I already told him," Lisa said carefully. "But he insisted. He gave me his card."

Vijay sighed and finally lifted his eyes. The moment he read the name on the card, his heart stilled. His fingers tightened around the thin piece of paper.

It wasn't just anyone. It was the private detective he had quietly hired weeks ago; the man carrying answers Vijay wasn't sure he was ready to face.

He stood abruptly, his chair scraping against the polished floor.

"Send him in," Vijay ordered, his tone sharper than usual. He glanced at his team. "Continue without me. I'll rejoin later."

A ripple of surprise swept through the room. Vijay Chandel never abandoned meetings, not even for small matters or emergencies that others deemed urgent. His dedication was unshakable. The only times he left work were to return home for his daughter, Nisha.

But today, he walked out.

His people exchanged silent glances, wondering who this mysterious visitor could be. What could make their iron-willed leader abandon the very project he had called "the company's lifeline"?

Vijay didn't look back. He already knew this meeting was about to change everything, perhaps even reopen wounds he had buried for years.

***

Chapter 2
The Rain Outside, The Storm Within

The Chandel Estate glowed like a palace against the restless monsoon sky. Inside, chandeliers sparkled, and laughter spilled through the grand halls. Music drifted softly, blending with the sound of rain tapping against the tall glass windows. It was a magnificent riverside home, the Chandel Estate at Chiswick Mall, London, where the Thames glimmered just beyond the garden. Guests often paused at the balcony to admire the view, though tonight, all eyes were on Nisha.

It was a night of celebration. Nisha Chandel, the pride of her father, had completed her master's degree and was soon to join the company. Guests praised her charm, her intelligence, her future. Everyone seemed to smile for her.

Everyone, except Nisha herself.

She sat quietly by a tall window in the corner of the hall, her knees drawn close, her cheek pressed against the cool glass. Outside, silver streaks of rain blurred the garden lanterns. Their flames shivered in the wind, just as her heart trembled with unspoken thoughts.

To the world, she was the daughter of a powerful man. To herself, she was a young woman caught between duty and desire.

Her father noticed. Vijay Chandel had learned to read silence as easily as he read numbers on a business chart; that silence had raised his suspicion.

Later that evening, he called her into his study. Away from the laughter, the soft glow of a lamp warmed the quiet room.

"My sweet pea," he said gently, using the nickname only he called her, "why does your smile look so heavy tonight? This should be your happiest day. Tell me, what's troubling you?"

Nisha hesitated, biting her lip. For a moment, she wished she could stay silent. But her father's eyes, calm, steady, yet filled with love, drew the truth from her.

"Dad… there's a boy," she whispered. "Someone I met in college. I like him... a lot. But I don't know how he feels about me. Sometimes I think he might care… but other times, I doubt it."

Vijay leaned back, a faint smile playing on his lips. "Ah… so it's not just liking, is it? You're in love."

Her cheeks flushed, and she looked down.

He placed a hand on her shoulder. "Listen, my sweet pea. If you truly care for him, tell him. Be honest with your heart. If he loves you, your world will be brighter than ever. And if he doesn't…" his voice softened, carrying a weight she could not yet understand, "…then it's his loss. But never chain your heart in one-sided love. That curse is hard to carry. Once it enters, it stays for a lifetime."

Nisha studied her father's face, surprised by the gravity in his voice. "Dad… how do you know that so well?"

For a moment, his gaze drifted somewhere far away, to a past she had never seen. His eyes shimmered with memories, and his smile was tinged with pain.

"If you fail, my daughter," he whispered, "then I will tell you my own story. A story of love that never found its way."

He tightened his grip gently on her shoulder. "But not tonight. Tonight belongs to you. Go, enjoy the evening. Remember always, you are my sweet pea, my greatest pride."

Nisha nodded slowly, though her heart still felt heavy. She walked out of the study, leaving her father alone in the dim light.

And in that silence, Vijay closed his eyes. For the first time in years, the ghost of his past love stirred again, demanding to be remembered.

***

Chapter 3
The Name That Still Hurts

The house had gone quiet. Guests had left, music had faded, and the storm outside had softened into a gentle drizzle.

In his study, Vijay sat alone in the leather chair, the lamp casting a pale glow across his tired face. His phone lay in his hand, unlocked, as though it had been waiting all these years for this moment.

With a slow breath, he opened the gallery. And there she was.

Venus.

The photograph was old, blurred at the edges, yet her smile remained untouched by time. The kind of smile that could light up the darkest sky. The kind that had once been his strength and later, his curse.

His fingers trembled as he touched the screen. His powerful hands, ones that had signed million-dollar deals without hesitation, now shook because of a single face.

A single name.

"Venus…" he whispered, his voice cracking like glass.

The word left his lips like a prayer, fragile and broken. Tears welled in his eyes, sliding down his cheeks before he could stop them. For years, he had buried this love beneath his work, his responsibilities, and his role as a father. But tonight, the memories returned.

Memories of her laughter. Memories of the way her eyes held worlds he could never reach. Memories of standing close enough to feel her warmth, yet never close enough to call her his.

One-sided love. The curse he had warned Nisha about. The curse he had carried like a silent wound in his chest.

He leaned back, closing his eyes, letting the tears fall freely now. The storm outside had left the sky, but inside him, the storm had only begun again.

"Venus," he whispered once more, softer this time, as though speaking directly to the ghost of her soul.

And in that quiet night, with nothing but rain dripping from the eaves, the mighty Vijay Chandel—business tycoon, father, leader—became just a man, broken by a love that never chose him.

***

Chapter 4
The Winter She Appeared

The first time Vijay saw her, the air was sharp with winter cold. The university campus in North India was wrapped in fog, its red-brick buildings half-hidden beneath a soft, milky veil. Students hurried past with steaming cups of tea, their laughter echoing in the crisp December air.

Vijay was a senior then, known for his discipline, ambition, and quiet resolve. His world revolved around books, projects, and the silent pressure of becoming someone worthy in life. Love had never crossed his mind; it was a distraction meant for others.

And then, she appeared.

Venus.

She walked across the college courtyard wrapped in a pale blue shawl, her hair catching tiny drops of dew. Her friends surrounded her, talking and laughing, but to Vijay, the world blurred. In that single moment, she was the only figure in focus.

Her laughter was soft, yet it carried through the air like music. Her eyes held a brightness that seemed to cut through the fog. And the way she tucked her hair behind her ear—it was the smallest gesture, yet it pulled at something deep in his chest.

He had seen many faces before, but never one that made him feel this sudden, unexplainable pull. *It wasn't love at first sight*, he told himself. No, it was something heavier, something that struck him without warning.

From that day onward, winter carried a new meaning for him.

Vijay began noticing her everywhere. In the library, her books spread wide as she scribbled notes in neat handwriting. In the cafeteria, sipping tea with her friends, her laughter rose above the noise. Even in the corridors, where the echo of her anklets would reach him before her presence did.

And he, who once lived with strict schedules and seriousness, found himself doing things he never imagined.

He began bunking classes.

Not because he disliked them, but because her path to the library passed the old banyan tree. If he timed it right, he could sit on the bench nearby, pretending to read a book, just to catch a glimpse of her walking past.

Sometimes he would sit for hours, watching groups of students move in and out, his heart tightening each time the blue shawl came into sight.

He knew it was foolish. And yet in those brief seconds, when she walked past without ever noticing him, the world felt brighter. She never knew, but those moments stitched themselves into the fabric of his days.

Then, one afternoon, the truth came like a blow.

He had followed the sound of her laughter to the back of the campus lawns. She wasn't alone. A boy was with her—a tall, confident junior—his hand brushing lightly against hers as they walked.

They stopped beneath a neem tree, speaking softly, and she looked at him with a tender smile, her eyes glowing with affection. Vijay's chest tightened painfully. It was the kind of smile he had dreamed of receiving but never would.

That evening, he couldn't bring himself to eat. The hostel mess buzzed with noise, but he sat still with his plate untouched. His friends joked and laughed, but their voices felt far away. Inside, something had cracked.

He had loved her silently, foolishly, selfishly, and without permission. And now, reality stood before him: Venus already belonged to someone else.

Still, the heart does not stop simply because it is told to.

So, Vijay continued his silent routine. He bunked classes not to dream of her love anymore, but just to see her smile from a distance. He told himself he wanted nothing more—that watching her be happy was enough.

But each night, when the hostel grew dark and the winter winds howled against the windows, he lay awake, whispering the same name into the silence.

"Venus."

And with every whisper, his heart bled a little more.

***

Chapter 4
The Winter She Appeared (Part II)

That night, when the hostel fell silent and the cold winds rattled the thin glass windows, Vijay lay staring at the ceiling. The laughter of Venus and that boy beneath the neem tree echoed in his mind like a haunting melody. No matter how hard he tried, he couldn't silence it.

His chest ached with the weight of a truth he could not change. She was not his, and she never would be.

He had two choices: let the pain destroy him, or bury it deep enough to live again.

The next morning, he chose the latter.

Vijay returned to his classes, forcing himself to sit through lectures he had once skipped. The banyan tree, the library corridor, the café corner, he avoided them all. He trained his eyes not to search for the blue shawl, not to wait for the sound of her anklets in the hallways.

He told himself, again and again, *she is not yours to think about*.

But forgetting Venus was not simple. Love does not disappear; it only hides in the quiet corners of the heart. So Vijay looked for ways to chain his restless thoughts, to drown them in something larger than himself.

That was when he found the theatre.

At first, it was accidental. A senior had dragged him into a small rehearsal hall, asking if he could help with props. Vijay agreed, thinking little of it. But when he stood in the shadows of the stage, watching actors pour out their souls in rehearsals, something inside him stirred.

Here was a place where emotions could be spoken freely. Where love, anger, pain, and joy were not weaknesses but art. Where a man could break on stage and still be applauded.

He began spending more and more time there, carrying props, learning lines when someone was absent. Slowly, he started performing small roles, losing himself in characters that weren't him.

Each time he acted, it felt as if he were emptying his own sorrow onto the stage. The applause did not erase the pain, but it gave it purpose.

And so, day by day, Vijay built a wall around his heart. On one side was Venus, untouchable, unreachable, forever smiling in memories. On the other side was his new self, the student, the worker, the dreamer of stages.

One-sided love had broken him. But it had also pushed him into a world where he would begin to build something greater than heartbreak: a calling, an identity, a future.

Still, when the night grew quiet, he found himself whispering her name into the silence.

"Venus..."

Not as a prayer anymore. But as a wound that would always remain.

***

Chapter 5
The Words Left Hanging

The rain had stopped, but the city still smelled of wet earth. Streetlights shimmered across damp pavement, and passing cars splashed puddles into the night air. Nisha walked slowly, her heart beating louder than the noise of traffic around her.

Her father's words echoed inside her:

"Don't live in a one-sided love, my sweet pea. Speak your truth."

She had promised herself she would do it tonight. No more waiting. No more fear.

She found him at the small coffee shop near the riverside, the one they had visited often as friends. The glass windows glowed warmly against the dark evening. Inside, he sat at their usual corner table, a notebook open before him, scribbling lines with a half-empty cup beside his hand.

For a moment, Nisha froze at the doorway. The world outside faded—the honking cars, the chatter of passersby, even the cool drizzle in the air. All she saw was him.

What if he didn't feel the same? What if this ruined everything?

But then her father's voice returned, gentle yet firm: *"Speak your truth."*

She took a deep breath and pushed the door open.

The bell above the café door chimed softly. He looked up, surprised, then smiled. "Hey, Nisha. Didn't expect you tonight."

She managed a faint smile, walking over to his table. The warmth of the shop couldn't calm the trembling in her chest. She pulled out the chair opposite him and sat down before her courage vanished.

"I… I wanted to tell you something," she said, her voice unsteady.

He closed his notebook and gave her his full attention. His eyes were kind, but that only made it harder.

Her palms were sweating. She swallowed hard, then forced herself to look straight at him.

"I like you, Rohan," she whispered, the words tumbling out. "Not just as a friend. I don't know when it happened, but you became… important to me. My days feel different because of you. I care about you, and I couldn't hide it anymore."

The café grew silent around her, or maybe it was only her heart drowning everything else out.

He blinked, stunned. For a second, his lips parted as though he might answer. Nisha held her breath, waiting for the reply that would either make her or break her.

And then, his phone rang.

The sharp sound cut through the air. He glanced at the screen, hesitated, then picked it up.

"Sorry… I have to take this," he said softly.

He stood and turned slightly away, his voice low as he spoke into the phone. Nisha sat frozen, her confession still hanging in the air between them, unanswered.

Minutes passed, though they felt like hours. Outside, the drizzle began again, tapping gently on the café windows.

When he finally ended the call, he gave her a small, unreadable smile. “I’ll… talk to you later, okay?”

And with that, he left, leaving her sitting alone at the corner table, her heart suspended between hope and despair.

Nisha lowered her eyes, her breath shaky. A tear slipped onto the table, disappearing into the damp wood before she could wipe it away.

“At least I said it,” she whispered to herself.

But deep inside, she knew this was only the beginning. The answer, the truth, was still waiting in the shadows of tomorrow.

And far away, in his study, her father opened an old diary, his fingers trembling as he touched the first page. The past, long buried, was finally ready to be told.

***

Chapter 6
Reflections in Silence

The night after the café felt longer than any Nisha had ever experienced.

She lay on her bed, her phone clutched tightly in her hand, the screen lighting up her anxious face again and again. But no message came. No call. Nothing. Only the quiet buzz of the city outside her window and the sound of her own breath, heavy and restless.

Her confession echoed in her ears: *"I like you... I care about you..."*

She replayed every word, every glance, every pause. Did he look surprised or uncomfortable? Did he smile, or had she imagined it? Did his silence mean rejection? Or was he simply caught off guard?

The more she thought, the heavier her chest felt. Loneliness crept into the corners of her room like a shadow. For the first time in years, she felt utterly small in a world that seemed too vast.

Morning brought no answers.

Her alarm rang, and she rose, mechanically preparing for her first week at her father's company. The mirror reflected her pale face and tired eyes. She dabbed on makeup, but nothing could hide the emptiness beneath.

At the office, congratulations poured in. Employees smiled warmly, welcoming her as the heir to the Chandel empire. She smiled back, polite and gracious, but inside she felt hollow. Her mind kept drifting to a single question: *Would he ever call?*

Her phone vibrated once. Her heart leapt only to sink again. A calendar reminder. Not him.

She slipped the phone back into her bag and forced herself to listen to the meeting, though every word felt like static.

Vijay noticed.

From his corner of the boardroom, he watched his daughter with quiet eyes. The world saw her as strong, intelligent, radiant. But a father sees what others cannot.

He saw the way her hands trembled slightly when she touched her phone. He saw the distant look in her eyes, as though part of her was trapped elsewhere. He saw the heaviness in her smile, one that had always been pure, but now seemed weighed down by invisible chains.

Vijay didn't ask. He didn't need to. He recognized the signs too well.

For years, he had carried that same silence in his own chest. He knew the taste of waiting for words that might never come, of staring at a phone as though it held the power to heal or destroy. He knew the curse of hope that refused to die, even when reason begged it to.

It was like watching his own reflection walk before him, only this time, it was his daughter living the ache.

That evening, as Nisha sat in her room again, staring blankly at her phone, Vijay knocked softly on her door.

"Sweet pea," he said, stepping inside. "How was your first day?"

She looked up, startled. "It was... fine."

But he heard the tremor in her voice. He sat beside her, not pressing, not questioning. For a while, they simply sat in silence, the air heavy with words unspoken.

Finally, he spoke, his voice low. "Waiting for someone's answer can feel heavier than silence itself. Like your heart is carrying a weight it was never built for."

Nisha blinked, her eyes stinging. "Dad..."

He placed a hand gently over hers. "I know, my sweet pea. I know."

She didn't ask how he knew. Something in his tone told her that her father had lived this before. And though he didn't share his story, she felt the unspoken truth that her pain was not hers alone.

That night, after Vijay left her room, Nisha sat by the window, watching the city lights blur in the drizzle. Her chest still ached, her heart still confused, her mind still replaying the unanswered moment at the café.

But in her father's words, she had found a fragile comfort. A reminder that even in loneliness, she was not completely alone.

Yet the question remained, pressing against her heart like a blade: *Would he answer?*

And if he did... would she be ready to hear it?

***

Chapter 7
The Answer

The message came late at night.

Nisha had been staring at her phone for hours, her eyes burning, her thoughts spiraling into darker corners. Just when she had begun to lose hope, the screen lit up.

Her heart leapt. It was from Rohan Mehra.

Her fingers shook as she unlocked the phone, reading the words that had been both her greatest wish and her greatest fear.

"Can we meet tomorrow? I think we should talk. Meet me at The River Café tomorrow evening at 7 o'clock."

She read it again. And again. Relief and dread twisted together inside her. Finally, she would know. But did she want to?

The next day crawled painfully. At home, her thoughts circled endlessly. Every hour felt longer than the last. She tried to read, to work, even to talk with her father, but nothing held her attention. Her mind replayed the moment over and over: What would Rohan say? Would he smile, turn her away, or even remember the depth of her words? By evening, her chest was constrained with both hope and fear, as though the river outside carried her heartbeat in its flow. The street buzzed with traffic, warm lights spilling across the pavement. Nisha arrived early, her hands cold, her breath uneven. Every passing minute only deepened her fear.

Then he walked in.

Her heart stuttered. He carried no books this time, no easy smile. His face was serious, his eyes guarded.

"Nisha," he said softly, pulling out the chair opposite her.

She managed a faint smile. "Thanks for coming."

For a moment, silence stretched between them. The clinking of cups, the chatter of strangers, the hum of the café all seemed distant. Only their eyes held the weight of the world.

Finally, he spoke. His voice was calm, but each word struck her chest like a stone.

"I don't want to hurt you. You're one of the most amazing people I've ever met. But..." He paused, exhaling as though the sentence itself was a burden. "...I don't feel the same way."

The words fell like glass shattering in her heart.

Nisha forced a smile, though her lips trembled. "I... I understand."

"No, please," he said quickly, guilt flickering across his face. "I didn't mean to make things difficult. I just... I don't want to give you false hope. You deserve more than that."

She nodded, her throat burning. Her hands gripped the edge of the table so tightly that her knuckles turned white. Inside, she was breaking, but outside, her voice stayed steady.

"It's okay," she whispered. "Thank you for being honest."

The café blurred around her. His words echoed again and again: "*I don't feel the same way.*"

She excused herself quickly, unable to bear another second of the pity in his eyes.

Outside, the evening air was cool, but to her it felt suffocating. Cars honked, people hurried past, but she walked without seeing anything, her steps uneven, her breath sharp and shallow.

It felt like the whole city was moving forward while she was frozen in place. Every noise, every light, every shadow reminded her of the storm inside her chest.

When she finally stopped walking, she found herself by the riverside. The water rushed quietly in the dark, indifferent to her pain. She stood there for a long time, her tears falling silently, her body heavy with the weight of words she had prayed never to hear.

Her father's warning whispered back to her: *"One-sided love is a curse you can't remove easily."*

Now she understood. Now she felt its truth carved into her heart.

That night, when she returned home, Vijay was waiting in the study. He looked up, and in her face, her swollen eyes, her trembling lips, he saw the answer without needing to ask.

For a long moment, they said nothing. Then, as if words were too small for such pain, Nisha fell into his arms.

Vijay held her close, his hand steady against her back, though his own eyes glistened. He knew this ache. He knew it too well.

And in that quiet, as the city outside carried on, father and daughter were bound together by the same wound—two hearts scarred by the same curse of love unreturned.

***

Chapter 8
A Sudden Winter

The change in Nisha Chandel was impossible to ignore.

It did not creep slowly, the way time changes a face or seasons fade into each other. It came like a storm in the night: sudden, startling, and complete. One evening, she had been the girl who smiled easily and carried warmth in her words. By the next morning, she was someone else entirely.

Her colleagues felt it first. In the boardroom, Nisha's tone sharpened. She cut through weak arguments like a blade, her voice firm, her eyes unwavering. Decisions that once took her days now came in minutes. She no longer dressed her words with softness; she spoke them as they were: unpolished, final.

"Cold," they whispered among themselves. "Too cold..."

And yet, when crisis struck, she was the first to act.

When a junior stumbled during a major presentation, she dissected his errors with surgical precision, but later coached him patiently until he stood confident again. When a staff member's family faced eviction, she handled the paperwork personally, ensuring they kept their home.

When a secretary's daughter needed expensive surgery, it was Nisha who made the call to the hospital, her voice steady, commanding, leaving no room for hesitation: *"Send the bill to the company. It will be handled."*

Her contradictions unsettled everyone.

How could the same woman, who dismissed a proposal without a second glance, also spend hours helping a struggling intern prepare for the next one? How could she be cold in her words but warm in her actions?

No one could answer. They only saw that she had changed, and they had not been ready for it.

It was in her eyes that the transformation was most visible.

They no longer carried the hopeful gleam of a young woman waiting for life to surprise her. They were calm, distant, almost guarded as though they had seen enough in silence to learn not to expect. When people tried to step closer, they were met with a polite wall.

She was courteous, yes. Respectful, always. But never open. Never inviting.

The warmth of love, the innocence of attachment, had disappeared from her gaze. And though no one spoke of it aloud, everyone felt the loss of something they could not name.

Vijay noticed more than anyone.

He watched his daughter with quiet eyes, reading the changes others only speculated about. He saw her decision-making harden, her laughter fade, her friendships narrow into silence. He saw her treat people fairly, with dignity, sometimes with more kindness than she revealed.

But he also saw the wall she had built around herself.

A wall he knew too well.

At night, when the estate fell into silence, he thought of the sudden 360-degree turn in her nature. He wondered how much pain a heart must carry to shift so completely, so suddenly. He wondered if she would ever let that wall fall or if it would grow taller with time.

The world looked at Nisha with awe.

Some admired her strength, her clarity, her fearlessness. Others whispered of her coldness, her detachment, her ruthless focus. But all agreed on one thing: she was not the same woman they had once known.

What had caused the change, no one could say.

It was as though a winter had settled into her heart overnight, turning warmth to frost, tenderness to steel.

And yet, beneath that ice, when the moment called for it, she still lit fires of kindness that surprised even those closest to her.

She had become a mystery, a woman both cold and compassionate, untouchable yet indispensable.

And the question lingered, heavy and unspoken, in every room she entered:

What happened to Nisha Chandel?

***

Chapter 9
Words She Couldn't Speak

The house was silent that night.

Nisha sat at her desk, her lamp glowing faintly against the dark. The files from the office lay untouched beside her. Instead, her hand moved across the pages of a worn leather journal.

On these pages, she was not the sharp executive her colleagues knew. She was not the cold, detached woman people whispered about. Here, she was simply herself: raw, fragile, unguarded.

Her pen scratched against the paper, shaping words that felt too heavy to keep inside:

"Love is not a promise; it is a question.

You answer it with your trust,

and sometimes the answer comes back empty.

It is the silence that hurts more than the rejection."

She paused, staring at the words until her eyes blurred. Then she turned the page and wrote again:

"Hearts don't break with noise.

They break quietly,

like glass slipping from the hand

before it even hits the floor."

She closed her eyes, her chest tightening as memories slipped through her mind. The café. His silence. The final words: *"I don't feel the same way."*

To the world, she had erased those moments. But here, in her journal, they lived on bleeding into poems, shaping themselves into short stories of love found and lost.

One of her stories filled the next few pages:

The Girl at the Window

"There was once a girl who waited by a window every evening. She never told anyone why.

People thought she was waiting for the sunset, or for the stars to appear.

But she was waiting for footsteps,

for a familiar face that never came.

She grew tired of waiting. One day, she shut the window.

And though the world kept moving,

the girl never looked outside again."

Nisha's hand trembled as she finished. She closed the journal halfway, pressing her forehead against it. The silence of her room echoed with the voices of her own words.

The door creaked softly.

Vijay stepped inside, his footsteps measured. "Sweet pea," he said gently, "you didn't come down for dinner. I thought I'd check on you."

Nisha lifted her head quickly, startled. "Dad… I was just… " She pushed the journal aside, but in her rush, the pages remained open.

Vijay smiled faintly, moving closer. "Working too hard again?"

As he spoke, his eyes fell upon the open pages. At first, he intended to look away. He had never believed in stepping into another's private world unless invited. But the words caught his eye before he could stop himself.

"Hearts don't break with noise.

They break quietly..."

His breath stilled. Against his will, his eyes drifted further.

"...like glass slipping from the hand

before it even hits the floor."

He froze. For a moment, the study around him blurred. The words pulled him somewhere else, into memories he had buried, into wounds he had stitched but never healed.

Venus.

The name echoed in the silence of his mind.

He closed the journal gently, his hand trembling against the leather cover.

Nisha looked at him, unsure whether he had read anything. But his eye told her enough. There was a weight in them, a shadow of the past she had never been told.

"Get some rest, my sweet pea," he said softly, his voice lower than usual.

And as he left the room, carrying the echo of her words inside him, he realized something with aching clarity:

Her pain had awakened his own.

***

Chapter 10
The Whisper of a Name

The study was silent. Only the low hum of the table lamp filled the stillness of the night. Vijay sat with Nisha's journal open before him, though his eyes were no longer on her words. His fingers rested on the fragile paper as though it carried a weight he could not lift.

For a long moment, he stared at the tremble of his own hands. Then rose and walked to the mirror across the room. The man who stared back at him was in his mid-forties, his face calm on the surface but his eyes carrying storms no one else could see.

"Venus..." The name slipped out of his lips like a broken prayer.

His reflection blurred as tears swelled, making the edges of the mirror indistinct. It was as if the glass itself refused to bear the weight of his truth. He closed his eyes, and the darkness pulled him back—not to his college years, not to the distant past—but to a day that still clung to him like an open wound.

Five years after college...

Vijay had been in Greater Noida, wandering through a mall glittering with neon lights and the clamor of weekend shoppers. Music from nearby stores bled into one another, laughter echoed off the walls, and the scent of coffee and popcorn filled the air. For him, it was just another ordinary day.

Until he saw her.

Venus.

She stood near a clothing store, her fingers brushing against fabrics, a bag hanging lightly from her arm. The sight struck him like lightning. For a moment, his entire world froze. The noise of the mall dimmed, his breath caught, and the faint smile he had been wearing disappeared as though it had never existed.

His eyes burned, filling with tears before he could even understand what was happening. The years between them vanished in an instant. It was as though time itself had conspired to remind him of the ache he thought he had left behind.

Venus looked radiant, her face lit with the same effortless grace that once turned days into dreams for him. She laughed gently at something the shop assistant said, the sound drifting through the air and striking him like an arrow. To her, it was just another day, another errand. To him, it was the reopening of an old wound.

He wanted to call her name, to step forward, to let out everything he had carried in silence. But his body betrayed him, his feet rooted to the floor, his voice trapped in his throat. All he could do was stand there, trembling, with tears threatening to fall.

And so, he turned away.

His vision blurred as he walked quickly through the crowd, head lowered, trying to escape before his heart shattered in front of strangers. Each step was heavier than the last, his chest constricted, his mind screaming her name though his lips remained shut.

That night, he had sat alone in his room, staring at the ceiling in darkness, the echo of her laughter still tearing through him. He had thought time would heal him, but Greater Noida proved otherwise. Her presence, even from a distance, had undone everything.

The memory collapsed into the present.

Vijay opened his eyes, staring once more at his reflection. His face was wet, his breath ragged. The room around him was still the same, but inside, he was back in that mall, back in that moment where his smile vanished and his heart broke silently all over again.

With trembling fingers, he closed Nisha's journal and held it against his chest. The irony was not lost on him: his daughter pouring her heartbreak into words, while his own had lived buried in silence for decades. He looked at the mirror one last time. "Venus," he whispered again, his voice a mix of longing and despair, a name that had never left him.

The night held his secret, just as it always had.

***

Chapter 11
The Shadows That Follow

Vijay Chandel's eyes darted across the files strewn over the conference table. Around him, his team spoke in measured tones, discussing strategies, projections, and contingencies for a project that could define the company's future. Every detail mattered, every number, every plan. This meeting was the pulse of the empire he had built, and he was at its center, analyzing, directing, and calculating.

A soft knock at the door interrupted the discussion. Lisa stepped in, her voice cautious.

"Sir... someone is here to see you."

Vijay didn't look up immediately. "Ask him to wait. I'm busy," he said, his tone clipped but controlled.

Lisa hesitated, then extended a card. "He insisted... and he gave me this."

Vijay's eyes fell on the name. Recognition hit him instantly, a jolt that made the air in the room feel heavier. His grip tightened around the pen. Without another word, he stood abruptly, the chair scraping against the polished floor.

"Take him to my personal cabin. I'll be there in a moment," he ordered, voice sharper than usual.

The team exchanged glances, a ripple of surprise passing among them. Vijay Chandel never left a meeting, especially not one this critical. Yet today, he walked out without a second thought.

The corridors of Chandel Enterprises were quiet as Vijay moved with purpose. Evening had settled over the city; the skyline outside glowed softly against the darkening sky. Each step toward his personal cabin was deliberate, measured, but underneath that calm exterior, a storm of anticipation churned.

He opened the door. The detective was already seated, calm, sharp-eyed, carrying the quiet weight of someone who had seen too much and survived. The moment Vijay closed the door behind him, the air shifted. Corporate calm dissolved into a private intensity that demanded attention.

The detective slid an envelope across the polished table. Vijay took it without hesitation. The weight was more than physical; it carried meaning, urgency, and the hint of danger.

Inside was a photograph: a jagged island, waves crashing against its cliffs, a lone man standing at the edge. Coordinates were written neatly at the bottom. A name, scrawled in hurried handwriting, suggested secrecy and peril.

Vijay studied the photograph silently. "Is this certain?" he asked, voice sharp but contained.

"As certain as I can be," the detective replied. "But certainty does not guarantee safety."

Vijay pressed further. "Who sent this?"

The detective's gaze remained steady. "Not everyone wants the truth uncovered. Some will kill to keep it hidden."

Vijay folded the photograph slowly, slipping it into his coat pocket. His face remained composed, but a slight tremor betrayed the crack in his usually unshakable control.

"And one more thing," the detective added, leaning back slightly. "This wasn't delivered to me directly. Someone left it where I would find it... as if they wanted me to bring it to you."

Vijay's pulse quickened. Unknown forces pulling strings in the shadows. Was this a guide or a trap?

"The coordinates... that place changes people," the detective continued. "Answers may be there, but they do not come cheap."

Vijay remained silent, staring at the city skyline beyond the cabin window. A low, broken sigh escaped his lips. He was deep in a labyrinth, each revelation only creating new questions, each clue twisting into another mystery.

His phone buzzed. A message flashed from an anonymous number:

"You think you know, but you do not. He is already watching."

Vijay's heartbeat quickened. The photograph, the detective, the cryptic message, they formed a web of shadows that tightened around him. And just like that, the evening that began in the conference room had transformed into the first step of something far larger, far darker, and far more dangerous.

Vijay remained staring at the city skyline, the weight of the photograph pressing against his mind. The detective's words echoed, each one heavier than the last. *"The coordinates... that place changes people. Answers may be there, but they do not come cheap."*

He folded the photograph carefully and slipped it into his coat pocket, feeling its weight as though it carried more than paper, perhaps a warning, a promise. His face remained composed, but his hand trembled ever so slightly, a crack in his usually unshakable control.

The detective rose, moving toward the door with measured steps. "When you decide to go... do not go alone," he said, his voice low but deliberate, each word hanging in the room.

The cabin door closed behind him, and silence returned, but it felt different now. Heavy. Pregnant with anticipation. Vijay could still hear the faint echo of the detective's words lingering in the air, mingling with the hum of the city outside.

He reached for his phone almost instinctively but paused. Another message flashed on the screen, anonymous, brief, and chilling:

"Do not trust the obvious. What you see is only a shadow of the truth."

Vijay's heartbeat quickened. Every instinct in him screamed caution, but curiosity, the old familiar drive, pulled him forward. He knew the detective had delivered something far bigger than just a photograph; it was the first piece of a puzzle that could either save or destroy everything he had built.

He leaned against the table, closing his eyes briefly. The name on the photograph, the coordinates, the cryptic warnings, it all felt too deliberate, too precise, as though someone had planned this moment long before he had even walked into the cabin.

A faint noise from outside drew his attention. Footsteps? Or just the building settling in the quiet evening? His mind raced. Every shadow seemed to move; every creak sounded like a signal. His senses sharpened.

Vijay pulled the photograph from his pocket again, studying it in the dim light. The island's jagged cliffs and the lone figure standing at its edge all seemed symbolic—almost like a mirror to the isolation he had felt all these years—making him wonder if the man on the island had already gone through the same journey he was about to begin.

He traced the coordinates with his finger, memorizing them. Something about the way the numbers were written, hurried yet precise, made him suspect this was only the surface of a larger secret.

The thought of the detective lingered at the back of his mind. Was he helping? Or had he been manipulated into delivering this message? Vijay had learned long ago that people's motives were rarely pure, and no one ever acted without reason.

He put the photograph down and walked toward the window, the city lights reflecting in his eyes. He whispered under his breath, a quiet acknowledgment of the unknown forces at play:

"Who are you… and why now?"

For a long moment, there was no answer. Only the hum of the city, the distant sound of traffic, and the soft flicker of lights in the office. But the unease did not fade; it grew heavier, pressing against him like the tide of the waves crashing in the photograph.

Vijay's mind began racing. The detective had said the place changes people. Answers do not come cheap. Who else knew about this? Was the man in the photograph alive or already gone? Was the message meant to lure him into danger or to save him from something far worse?

Vijay's jaw tightened. The room, quiet moments ago, now seemed alive with unseen eyes, silent and observing. He could feel it: a faint weight of presence, as though the shadows themselves carried secrets meant only for him.

He took a deep breath and straightened up. His hands gripped the edge of the table. This was no longer about curiosity or caution. It was about survival, about unraveling a puzzle deliberately left for him, piece by piece.

Vijay realized that the photograph, the detective, the messages were not just clues. They were strands of a web, and he was at its center. Each decision, each step forward, could reveal a truth or trap him further in uncertainty.

And yet, despite the growing tension, he felt the familiar fire ignite inside him—the fire that had built Chandel Enterprises from the ground up. He would not turn back. He could not.

His eyes fell once more on the photograph, and he whispered, a quiet but resolute vow:

"I will find him. And I will know the truth."

A soft flicker of movement caught his attention from the corner of the room. For a fraction of a second, he thought he saw a shadow that did not belong to the lights, a figure just at the edge of perception. He blinked, and it was gone.

The cabin was silent again, but the tension had doubled. Every sound, every flicker of light, every thought in his mind became charged with suspicion. Someone, somewhere, was orchestrating this. And Vijay knew, with the certainty only experience could teach, that this was only the beginning.

He turned back to the photograph one last time, memorizing the coordinates, the shape of the island, the lone figure. Whoever had placed this here wanted him to act, but what they hoped he would do remained unknown.

The room seemed to hold its breath, as if waiting for him to make the next move. And Vijay Chandel, unshaken in the boardroom, unshakable in his empire, now faced a different kind of challenge—one of shadows, secrets, and questions that refused to be answered easily.

Tonight, the game had begun. And somewhere in the darkness, the first pieces were already moving.

Vijay stood motionless for a long moment, the city lights stretching like veins across the darkness outside the cabin window. He could hear the faint hum of the office ventilation, the subtle creak of the building settling. But even familiar sounds felt charged, as though the very walls of Chandel Enterprises were alive with anticipation.

The photograph in his pocket seemed to pulse against his chest, a silent heartbeat that matched his own. He reached down, pulling it out and spreading it across the table once more. The man on the island stood rigid, shoulders squared against some invisible force. The wind, the waves, the desolate cliffs, they all seemed to whisper something he could not yet understand.

He traced the coordinates with a fingertip, imagining the location as though he could step into it through sheer will. The numbers were precise, almost clinical, but the handwriting of the name, jagged and hurried, betrayed emotion and urgency. Someone had wanted this to be found. Someone had wanted him to see it.

A flicker of movement at the edge of the cabin caught his attention. His heart skipped. Shadows shifted in the corners of his vision. He blinked, and nothing was there. Yet the unease remained, crawling along his spine, whispering that he was being watched.

He leaned back in the chair, the leather creaking under his weight. Memories surfaced, unbidden. He thought of all the times he had chased certain numbers, contracts, and strategies, and realized how fragile it all was. Even his empire, built brick by brick, rested on calculated assumptions. But this... this was different. The rules were unknown, and the stakes were personal.

Vijay's phone buzzed again, pulling him from his reverie. Another message, cryptic and unnerving:

"The closer you get, the less you can trust. Everything is a shadow."

He exhaled slowly, letting the tension drain for just a moment. Shadows. Truths hidden in plain sight. A trap laid meticulously for someone clever enough to follow the threads and yet bold enough to walk straight into them.

His gaze returned to the photograph. The lone man on the island seemed almost alive, the waves crashing around him like a challenge. Vijay imagined himself there, the wind tearing at his coat, the cliffs dropping sharply into the churning sea. The image felt more than a clue; it was a call. A provocation.

The detective's warning echoed in his mind: "*Answers may be there, but they do not come cheap.*"

He pressed his fingers to his temple, trying to force clarity. Who had left the photograph? And why? The detective had delivered it, but he had made it clear he was merely a messenger. There were other players, other forces. Someone had wanted him to see it tonight, at this exact moment. But for what purpose?

Vijay stood and began pacing the cabin, the leather soles of his shoes scraping against the polished floor. He felt the weight of his empire behind him—all the decisions, all the power, yet none of it could prepare him for this unknown. In the conference room, he was invincible; here, alone with shadows and messages, he was exposed.

He stopped suddenly; the image of the island etched into his mind. Something about the figure's stance, the way he faced the sea, told Vijay that the man was waiting for something or someone. Was it a message for him? Or a warning he was too late to heed?

A sudden noise outside the cabin made him spin toward the door. A soft thump, almost imperceptible, then silence. His breath hitched. The office was supposed to be empty. Every instinct screamed that this was no accident.

He moved to the door, hand on the handle, and paused. The corridor was empty. Just the soft hum of electricity and the distant echo of the city. Yet the feeling persisted. Someone or something was watching.

Vijay returned to the table, laying the photograph flat. He picked up a pen and began to make notes: the coordinates, possible routes, the faint markings in the handwriting. Each notation felt like a thread, each thread pulling him deeper into the maze he could not yet see the edges of.

He paused again, a thought gnawing at him. The detective had warned him against going alone. But who could he trust? The message on his phone had warned him that everything could be a shadow. Even the detective, what if he's an ally or a pawn in a larger scheme?

The tension was almost unbearable. Every sound, every flicker of light, every shadow seemed to carry intent. And yet, despite the danger, despite the uncertainty, Vijay felt the old familiar fire ignite within him. He had faced impossible odds before. He had built empires, negotiated crises, and controlled chaos. That, whatever it was... was another challenge.

He spoke aloud, almost to test the sound in the room:

"I will find the truth. Whoever this is… I will know their purpose."

The silence responded with nothing, yet it felt heavy, as though the world was holding its breath, waiting.

Then a final message appeared on his phone, chilling and precise:

"The first step is taken. But the path is watched. Do not misstep."

Vijay's jaw tightened. Every instinct screamed caution, but every fiber of his being demanded action. This was no longer curiosity. This was necessity. The pieces were moving, the threads were tangled, and someone, somewhere, had set the stage for him to follow.

He leaned back in the chair, his mind racing. The detective, the photograph, the cryptic messages, they were not just clues. They were challenges. Tests. Shadows and lights, truths and lies, all woven into a puzzle only he could attempt to solve.

Vijay Chandel, master of empires, architect of control, now faced a new game. One where certainty was a lie, trust was a weapon, and every step could reveal the truth or destroy him.

And somewhere, beyond the reach of the cabin walls, the first move of the shadowed players had already begun.

***

Chapter 12
The Rival

The glass façade of Blackwood Global Holdings tower gleamed against the London night, its sharp lines cutting into the skyline like a blade. Inside the top floor, a long mahogany table stretched across a vast boardroom. Around it sat men and women in tailored suits, their faces illuminated by the pale glow of a presentation screen.

But none dared speak too loudly.

At the head of the table sat Edward Blackwood.

He was impeccably dressed in a black suit, his cufflinks catching the light with every subtle movement. His grey eyes were cold, calculating, and his presence alone commanded silence.

A report had just been read out. It wasn't good.

"Decline of eight percent in publication revenues this quarter," a director said nervously, her voice barely above a whisper. "Two major authors have moved their contracts elsewhere. The last three book launches failed to recover costs. And…" She paused, glancing at Edward, "…the flagship project that was expected to balance these losses has been transferred to Chandel Enterprises. Under Mr. Vijay Chandel."

The room grew colder.

Edward leaned back in his chair, steepling his fingers. His lips curved into something that might have been a smile, but it never reached his eyes.

"So," he said slowly, his voice calm but cutting, "not only do we bleed money, but our last chance of patching the wound has been handed… to him."

Silence. The directors looked at one another, but no one answered.

Edward rose from his chair, moving toward the glass wall that overlooked the city. From here, the Thames wound its way through London, dark and endless. His reflection stared back at him, tall, commanding, unreadable.

Eight years.

It had been eight years since the humiliation that had marked him. Eight years since he had walked into his father's company as the heir to a dynasty, eager to prove himself with his first project. He had worn the same black suit, stood in another boardroom, and promised that he would deliver. That project was supposed to establish him, to announce to the world that Edward Blackwood was worthy of the name.

Instead, it had been taken from him.

Taken because the board believed he wasn't capable. Taken because a newcomer, an outsider, had shown more competence, more brilliance, more fire.

Vijay Chandel.

The name still tasted bitter on his tongue.

That first loss had cut him to the bone. He had smiled in public, told the press it was a joint decision, but inside, Edward had burned. And the fire had never gone out.

Now, eight years later, history had repeated itself. Another flagship project, a venture that was meant to stabilize Blackwood Global Holdings and revive its faltering divisions, had been taken from him and given to Vijay.

Edward's grip tightened on the glass railing. He remembered the news articles. The headlines had praised Vijay: *"Chandel Enterprises to Lead Revolutionary Project."* His own name had barely been mentioned, except as a footnote: *"Blackwood Global Loses Bid."*

He turned back to the table.

"Tell me," he asked softly, "why should I keep any of you?"

The directors shifted uncomfortably. No one spoke.

Edward walked back slowly, his footsteps deliberate, echoing in the silent room. He stopped near the presentation screen, his hand brushing over the declining graphs as if erasing them with his touch.

"Do you know what the world sees when they read these numbers?" he asked. "They see weakness. They see cracks in the foundation. They smell blood."

He paused, his eyes sweeping over the room.

"And predators," he continued, "do not forgive weakness."

One of the older directors, braver than the rest, cleared his throat. "Sir, perhaps if we focus resources on the publication arm..."

Edward cut him off with a raised hand. His voice remained calm, but steel threaded through it. "Blackwood Press International was once the crown jewel of this company. The name carried weight. Our authors defined culture, our newspapers shaped opinion, our books stayed in print for decades. And now?" He turned sharply, his eyes narrowing. "Now we lose talent to smaller houses, to companies run by men who should have been clerks in our offices, not competitors."

The words hung heavy. Everyone knew who he was referring to.

Vijay Chandel.

Edward sat down again, every movement controlled, precise. He leaned forward, elbows resting on the table.

"Do you know why he wins?" he asked, his tone dropping to a dangerous quiet. "Because he has nothing to lose. He builds his empire on hunger, on scars, on silence. And you," his gaze swept the room like a blade, "...you hand him victory by being blind, by being slow, by being ordinary."

The director who had spoken earlier lowered his eyes.

Edward exhaled slowly, regaining his calm. He reached for a glass of water, took a measured sip, and set it down.

"This project," he said at last, "was supposed to be mine. Eight years ago, the same thing happened. Do you remember what the papers said then? That I was too young, too inexperienced, not fit to carry my father's legacy." He smiled faintly, though it was bitter. "And do you know what hurt more than the words? The truth in them."

A long silence followed.

"But today," Edward continued, his voice cold, "there is no such excuse. Today, I am not inexperienced.

I am not untested. I am not weak. Yet once again, it is him."

He pushed his chair back, rising slowly. The directors held their breath.

"You want to talk about publication losses? About falling revenues? About failed launches?" He shook his head. "No. What we should be talking about is survival. Because if we do not rise now, if we do not strike when it matters, Chandel Enterprises will not only lead," his voice dropped, "it will consume."

The last word hit like a hammer.

Edward turned away again, walking back to the glass wall. His reflection waited for him there, cold and proud. The city stretched before him, full of lights, but he saw only one shadow: the shadow of a man he could not escape.

Vijay Chandel.

He whispered the name under his breath, his lips barely moving.

"You took the first project from me," he murmured, his voice low, meant for no one but himself. "You won't take the last."

Behind him, the directors sat in silence, unsure if the meeting was over, unsure if they were dismissed, unsure if they should even breathe.

Edward's hand slipped into his pocket, his fingers brushing over a silver pen, a gift from his father years ago, engraved with the Blackwood crest. He closed his hand around it, his knuckles whitening.

The battle was not over.

It had only just begun.

The room was silent, but Edward's mind raced. His reflection in the glass showed a man calm on the surface, but inside, fire and calculation burned fiercely. Blackwood Press International was bleeding. Not just in numbers, but in reputation. Every failed launch, every author lost, every scathing article in the press was a mark against the legacy his father had built.

Three major launches had collapsed in the last quarter alone. A bestselling author had walked away for a smaller, upstart company, citing "stifling management" and "lack of vision." Social media had erupted with critiques of Blackwood Press, questioning whether the once-great company could survive the next year. The headlines were merciless: *"Blackwood Press Loses Grip on Publishing," "Legacy in Decline," "From Glory to Ghost: The Fall of a Publishing Giant."*

Edward clenched his fist, feeling the weight of the failure in every fiber of his being. He had rebuilt this company from every setback, every loss, every betrayal, yet now, history threatened to repeat itself. Not because of incompetence, but because the very division meant to protect his legacy had become a liability.

He walked back to the table, running a hand along the polished mahogany. "This is not a minor crisis," he said quietly, almost to himself. "This is systemic. It's not just numbers. Its influence. It's culture. It's the voice of Blackwood being drowned out by hesitation and fear."

The directors sat frozen, sensing the change in his tone. Edward looked at each of them, his eyes sharp and demanding. "We have failed our authors. We have failed our readers. And most importantly, we have failed ourselves. Blackwood Press cannot continue in its current form. It is a liability. And a liability cannot fight a predator."

He turned back to the glass wall, looking out over the city as if seeking an answer in its sprawling lights. His reflection was not of a man defeated, but of a strategist preparing for a decisive move.

"I will sell Blackwood Press International," he said finally, voice steady, carrying a weight that allowed no argument. "Not because we cannot fight, but because this division cannot survive the way it is. I will select the buyer carefully, someone who can honor what we built, but also someone capable of striking at the world with precision where it matters."

He let the words linger, letting the weight of the decision sink in. The directors remained silent, their uncertainty mixing with awe.

"This is not surrender," Edward continued, pacing slowly. "This is strategy. This is survival. We cannot fight him here, not with this weakened, bleeding arm of our empire. But by selling it, by placing it in the hands of someone capable, we reclaim control. And we use what remains of Blackwood to strike where it counts."

He stopped near the presentation screen, fingers brushing over the declining revenue graphs as if erasing them from existence. "The world will see loss, yes. But loss can be a tool. Loss can be a weapon if wielded correctly. And when we strike, it will be with precision, and it will be with fire."

Edward exhaled slowly, regaining his calm. He turned to the directors, letting them feel the weight of his conviction. "Prepare the necessary steps. The sale will begin immediately. Every decision, every move, every negotiation will be mine to control. Blackwood Press International will no longer be a weakness. It will be part of the strategy that finally brings Vijay Chandel to his knees, not with brute force, but with the quiet inevitability of calculated power."

A hush fell over the boardroom. Even the most seasoned directors understood that this was no longer a routine decision; this was a statement. A declaration. Edward Blackwood was not finished.

He walked back to the window, gazing out at London, letting the cold night air in through the pane in his mind. The city was vast, indifferent, full of lights and shadows, but to Edward, it had narrowed down to one constant: the path to reclaiming what had been stolen.

"You took the first project from me," he murmured under his breath, eyes fixed on the darkness. "You will not take the last."

He straightened. His jaw set. The battle had shifted. The battlefield had changed. And the first move had been made. Blackwood Press International, once a symbol of pride and legacy, would now serve a higher purpose: the strategy, the weapon, and the fire that would ensure Edward Blackwood finally turned the tables.

The directors watched him, silently acknowledging that the war was no longer about revenue, about failed launches, or about criticism. The war was about survival, about control, about legacy. And Edward Blackwood had decided how to fight.

The city outside continued, unaware of the storm brewing in one of its most influential boardrooms. But inside, a plan had been set in motion. And when it unfolded, the world would remember the name Blackwood, not for failure, but for precision, power, and the quiet, unstoppable fury of a man who had waited eight years to strike back.

***

Chapter 13
The Silent Move

The office was quiet, the soft hum of the air conditioner filling the space with a low, constant drone. Outside, London's skyline glittered in the dying afternoon light, the Thames reflecting the city like molten silver. But Vijay Chandel's focus was not on the city; it was entirely inside the walls of his office, on the polished desk before him, on the papers, on the world he quietly controlled.

The door opened softly. Nisha stepped in, her heels clicking lightly against the polished floor, a stack of documents carefully held in her hands. She paused a moment, taking in the room, the organized precision, the faint scent of fresh ink, the subtle gleam of mahogany and glass.

"Dad," she said, her voice polite but warm as she set the documents down on the desk. "These are the contracts that need your signatures."

Vijay looked up from the papers he had been scanning. His sharp eyes softened slightly when they met hers, a small approving smile playing on his lips. "Nisha... I've been meaning to tell you something," he said. He leaned back in his chair, folding his hands. "I read your journals, the poems, the short stories you've been writing. Your writing... it's remarkable. Thoughtful, emotional, powerful. You put so much of yourself on paper; not many people can do that."

Nisha's lips curved in a small, polite smile. A faint blush touched her cheeks. "Thank you, Dad," she said quietly. "I... I never expected you to read them. I was just writing to express myself."

Vijay's eyes twinkled. "Expressing yourself is one thing, Nisha. But what you've written... It's beyond just expression. It's insight. You have a gift. Your words can move people, make them think, make them see themselves differently. That is rare. That is powerful."

She shifted slightly, embarrassed yet quietly proud. "I... I just write what I feel. I never thought it could mean much to anyone else."

Vijay leaned forward, resting his elbows on the desk. "That's exactly it. You don't write to impress; you write because it matters to you. That's why it resonates. Nisha... you have talent, real talent. Don't hide it. Don't let fear or doubt stop you from exploring it. One day, people will read your words and remember them. You could turn this into something more... something bigger. Something that belongs to you, entirely."

Nisha's eyes flickered with surprise. The thought of pursuing it professionally had never felt real before, and yet, hearing her father's words, it seemed possible. Exciting. "I... I appreciate your words, Dad. Truly. But my focus is elsewhere. My current work... it feels more pressing right now."

Vijay's smile softened. "I understand. Discipline is important. Priorities must be balanced. But remember this: discipline alone is not enough. Your creativity, your courage, your ability to put yourself into words... that is what sets you apart. Keep nurturing it. One day, it will matter in ways you can't even imagine."

Nisha nodded, feeling a surge of warmth and motivation. There was pride in his words, yes, but also challenge, a subtle push to grow, to reach, to believe. She placed her hand over the topmost contract. "I… I'll keep that in mind," she said softly.

Vijay's eyes lingered on her for a moment, assessing, approving, quietly proud. "Good. That's all I ask. And now… sign these, and let's make sure everything is in order here."

Nisha moved to collect her pens, the air between them filled with unspoken understanding. She felt lighter somehow, motivated, encouraged, ready to keep going, not for recognition, but because she had been reminded that her own voice mattered.

Before she could settle fully into her thoughts, the office door opened again. Lisa stepped in, her expression serious, her steps purposeful. "Sir," she said quietly, glancing at Vijay. "We need to talk. It's urgent."

Nisha's eyes narrowed slightly. There was something in Lisa's tone, a tension she couldn't ignore. "I'll step out then, Dad," she said politely, placing the documents down neatly. "I'll leave you both to it." She slipped out quietly, closing the door behind her, leaving the office almost silent.

Once the door clicked shut, the atmosphere in the room shifted. Vijay's calm demeanor sharpened, the subtle warmth of moments ago replaced by the cold precision of a man who controlled more than just his office.

"Lisa," he said, his voice low, controlled, and measured, "tell me everything."

Lisa nodded, leaning slightly forward. "Sir… Edward is planning to sell Blackwood Press International.

Secretly. Quietly, through layered negotiations. The deal isn't public; he's desperate to keep it hidden. He's moving fast, and if we don't act now, someone else could swoop in."

Vijay's lips curved into a faint, calculating smile. "I see." He leaned back, steepling his fingers. "We can acquire it… quietly, efficiently, without Edward even suspecting. Blackwood Press, the so-called crown jewel of Edward's empire. For decades, it had shaped opinion, published voices, and carried the Blackwood name across Europe. To sell it meant more than financial struggle; it meant surrender of identity."

"Are you certain?" Vijay asked finally.

"I have confirmation from a source inside Blackwood Global," Lisa continued, "wouldn't bring it to you otherwise. He's testing discreet buyers, hoping to close it before the market senses weakness. If this news leaks, Blackwood Global's image will collapse overnight."

Vijay was silent, Lisa waited for him to speak. She had worked for him long enough to know he valued silence before decisions.

At last, he spoke, his voice low, steady, calm.

"You will prepare to buy it," he said.

Lisa blinked. "In the company's name?"

"No," he said firmly. "Not in mine. Not in Chandel Enterprises. It will be under yours, Lisa. All paperwork, all transfers, everything. Later, when the time is right, we will move it. Once it's done, we can transfer it to Nisha." Vijay's sharp eyes glimmered with calculated certainty.

"Timing will be everything. Any leak could ruin the entire plan. We move carefully, decisively, and strategically. The company will belong where it should... in the right hands," he further explained.

Lisa hesitated, weighing each word. "Sir... the secrecy must be absolute. If Edward even suspects that I'm connected to you, he'll take extreme measures. We must ensure no paper trail, no meetings, no hints. Every step must look like it's just routine. Ordinary corporate movement."

Vijay nodded slowly, deliberately. "Exactly. Every transfer, every signature, every interaction must be unremarkable. Appearances are as important as the execution itself. We're playing a game of perception, Lisa. And perception, if controlled correctly, is power."

Lisa's eyes widened slightly, sensing the complexity of the chessboard laid before them. "Understood, sir. We can make it seamless. Quiet and precise."

Vijay leaned back, his gaze shifting to the city skyline beyond the glass walls. "Edward has underestimated us for far too long. He assumes weakness, distraction, mismanagement. But we are neither weak nor careless. We are patient, disciplined, and deliberate. That is the advantage we hold and the one we will exploit."

Lisa glanced at him, a flicker of admiration crossing her face. "Sir... with your guidance and careful planning, we can ensure this succeeds without risk of exposure. Nisha will take control, and Edward will remain blind to every move."

Vijay's expression softened ever so slightly. "Yes. And that is exactly how it must be. Everything must appear ordinary, predictable, mundane. Beneath that, the strategy unfolds. Quietly. Patiently. Efficiently. Until the moment we choose to reveal it... everything will already be set in place. By then, it will be irreversible."

Lisa exhaled, absorbing the careful weight of his words. The room was tense, but beneath the tension, there was a sense of clarity and purpose. They both knew that a single mistake could unravel months of planning. But they also knew that success would shift the balance of power irrevocably.

Vijay rose from his chair, moving to the window. The city stretched below him, its lights twinkling, unaware of the silent chess game unfolding above it. "Lisa... make sure every detail is accounted for. Every transaction, every contract, every move must be precise. No one sees, no one suspects, and no one interferes. Not Edward. Not anyone."

Lisa nodded, her determination solid. "I'll make it happen, sir. Quietly, without leaving a trace."

Vijay turned slightly, his eyes narrowing, voice low but sharp. "Good. And remember... the goal is not just to acquire a company. The goal is to secure the right future for it. Nisha must take control, completely and confidently. Everything else is just steps to ensure that she can do so without obstruction."

The office fell silent, except for the faint hum of the air conditioning and the distant city sounds below. A storm of strategy, secrecy, and anticipation had begun. And at its heart, the plan was simple yet bold: the acquisition must be invisible, the transfer flawless, and the ultimate beneficiary, Nisha, completely unaware to anyone else.

Vijay's eyes lingered on the skyline, on the city that pulsed beneath him. "This is just the beginning," he murmured to himself. "And by the time Edward realizes it, the game will already be over."

Outside, the city thrummed with its usual rhythm, oblivious to the quiet, calculated maneuvers being plotted in the office above. But within that room, a silent storm of strategy, suspense, and anticipation had begun a storm that would change the balance of power forever.

***

Chapter 14
The Grand Gambit

The December air in London was crisp, carrying that quiet chill that made the evenings feel longer than the days. At Chandel Enterprises, the corridors glowed under golden lights, and the rhythm of business carried on even as the rest of the city prepared for holidays. Inside Vijay Chandel's office, though, something entirely different was taking shape, a plan so silent and careful that no one beyond a handful of people even suspected it existed.

Lisa sat in her corner of the strategy department, papers neatly spread across her desk. Her laptop showed encrypted spreadsheets, coded transfers, and confidential reports. The name on the documents read L&S Holdings, a newly registered firm in Luxembourg. To anyone else, it was an ordinary European investment company. But Lisa knew better; it was a mask, a shell, a door through which Chandel Enterprises could move without leaving fingerprints.

She dialed a number, her voice calm and sharp at the same time. "Begin with the smaller shareholders," she instructed the broker. "Break it into pieces. No large orders. By the time anyone notices, we'll already have the control."

Blackwood Press International, the jewel of Edward Blackwood's empire, was crumbling under its own weight. Printing costs, poor digital growth, declining trust, all of it had left Edward with no choice but to look for buyers. But he wanted secrecy. If the market knew he was desperate, Blackwood Global's entire image would collapse.

Lisa, however, knew exactly where the cracks were. She began with the most vulnerable investors, those who had been frustrated for years. A few signatures here, a discreet transfer there, and the holdings started shifting quietly. No announcement, no alarms. Just silent movement on paper.

At the same time, Lisa's team approached creditors. Blackwood Press owed millions to private lenders. Edward had begged them for more time, but Lisa arrived with a different kind of offer, refinancing at better terms, but only if she controlled their claims. Desperation made the decision easy. Within days, the creditors agreed. Money speaks loudest when someone has run out of options.

By Christmas Eve, Lisa had quietly secured nearly sixty percent. The timing was intentional. London's financial world was distracted with holidays, deals slowed, analysts had gone home. But Lisa was still working, often until dawn, stitching together the threads of the plan.

Across the city, Edward Blackwood sat in his glass tower, his jaw tight as his CFO showed him the reports.

"There's unusual trading activity around the publishing arm," the man said cautiously. "Scattered names. Offshore accounts. It looks like accumulation of stake."

Edward's fingers tapped against the table. He didn't need to be told twice. "Who is behind it?"

The CFO hesitated. "It's impossible to trace for now. Whoever it is… they know how to hide."

Edward's gut twisted. He had fought enough battles to recognize the style. This was no random investor. This was Vijay. He didn't have proof, but he didn't need proof to know when an old enemy was circling.

"No," Edward muttered, his voice low but furious. "Not again."

He rushed to accelerate his own negotiations, calling discreet buyers, hoping to sell before control slipped from his hands. But everything worked against him: bureaucratic delays, nervous investors, and his own weakening credibility. Time was the one luxury Edward did not have, and time was exactly what Lisa and Vijay were stealing from him.

By mid-January, the silent accumulation was complete. Through proxies, through scattered brokers, through holding firms that looked ordinary, L&S Holdings now owned one hundred percent of Blackwood Press International.

When Edward finally ordered a full trace, the papers had already been signed, and the final minority shareholders had cashed their cheques. The company his father had built, the one he had sworn would always stay in Blackwood's hands, had been taken from him completely.

It was gone.

And the cruelest detail? Within seventy-two hours of the acquisition, Lisa transferred the ownership. Not to Vijay, not to Chandel Enterprises, but to Nisha. On paper, the publishing house now belonged to her. Clean, unquestionable, absolute.

The news broke publicly a week later. Newspapers carried the headline in bold:

"Blackwood Press Acquired in Full by L&S Holdings – New Vision Ahead."

The financial world lit up with speculation. Who was L&S Holdings? What would become of the famous press? And what did this mean for Edward Blackwood, once hailed the titan of publishing?

The answers came at a celebration no one expected.

At Chandel Estate, the mansion along the Thames, the chandeliers blazed with light, and the river shimmered outside like molten silver. Vijay had called it a "holiday gathering," but everyone knew it was more. Executives, writers, politicians, even rivals filled the halls, eager to witness what story the Chandel family would write next.

Nisha stood in the center, graceful but visibly surprised when Lisa handed her the official documents. Her fingers trembled slightly as she read them, her eyes widening.

"Papa..." her voice was almost a whisper. "This... this is mine?"

Vijay looked at her, his expression calm but proud. "It was always yours, Nisha. I only brought it to where it belonged."

For a moment, the noise of the party faded around her. She had written poems only to empty her heart, scribbled stories only to release pain. She had never imagined that her name would be tied to a publishing empire. Emotion welled in her chest, but she stood tall, blinking away the tears that threatened to show.

Edward, of course, was not there. His absence was louder than the music, louder than the speeches. Whispers floated across the ballroom about his silence, about his humiliation, about how quickly the mighty could fall.

Later that evening, while the orchestra played softly and glasses clinked, Vijay stepped out onto the balcony, watching the river reflect the city lights. Lisa joined him, her voice low.

"It's done. No trace leads back to us. The ownership is clear."

Vijay's gaze remained on the water. "Edward knows. He feels it in his bones. But suspicion without proof is weakness. And by the time he gathers his strength, it will be too late."

Lisa allowed herself a rare smile. "Nisha looked ready tonight. She carried it with grace."

"She doesn't know the weight yet," Vijay said quietly. "But she will. And when she does, she'll carry it as no one else can."

He raised his glass slightly, the river shimmering beneath the winter sky. "Edward thought the game was his. But the game has changed. And tonight, it has ended."

Inside, the party roared on, journalists scribbling notes, guests raising toasts, writers whispering about new opportunities. But beneath the music and laughter, everyone understood what had truly happened.

Edward Blackwood had lost.

Nisha had gained.

And Vijay Chandel, the man who never fought loudly, had won another battle in silence.

The city outside slept, unaware of the quiet war that had shifted its balance. But those who stood inside Chandel Estate that night would never forget, the true victories are the silent ones.

***

Chapter 15
The New Voice

The morning sky over London was pale and streaked with gold, the kind of light that promised clarity yet carried a chill of uncertainty. On the banks of the Thames, a new name glimmered across a freshly mounted glass panel: **Aurora Publishing House.**

The letters caught the light, elegant yet bold, as if declaring to the city that something unseen was being born. Where once the words "Blackwood Press International" had loomed, heavy and unyielding, now shimmered a name that spoke of beginnings.

Vijay Chandel stood in the main lobby, hands behind his back, watching workers finish polishing the marble floor. For him, this was more than another acquisition in his empire. This building was a vessel, meant not for profit alone but for something quieter and more lasting, a voice for those who had never been heard.

Lisa approached from the side, her heels sharp against the floor. A tablet rested in her hand, glowing with contracts, proposals, and lists of writers under consideration. "Everything is on schedule, sir," she reported, her tone clipped and efficient. "Renovations are complete, staff orientation begins tomorrow, and the first set of masterclass invitations has gone out."

Vijay nodded but didn't reply immediately. His gaze was fixed on the tall glass doors. Moments later, they opened, and Nisha walked in. Her pace was steady, her eyes moving over every detail as though the building itself were a page she needed to read.

She paused at the center of the lobby, her hand brushing the smooth railing of the staircase. For a moment, the silence between them stretched. She did not look like a guest here but like someone meant to belong here.

"This place," Vijay finally said, his voice carrying a quiet conviction, "will not be just a company. It will be a voice."

Nisha turned, her brows lifting. "A voice?"

"Yes," he answered, taking a slow step toward her. "Not mine. Not yours. Theirs. The ones no one has listened to. The ones who've been silenced, ignored, or forgotten. Aurora is for them."

The name seemed to echo faintly across the lobby. Lisa looked up from her tablet, intrigued, but remained silent.

Vijay's gaze softened when it met his daughter's. "You may not know this yet, Nisha, but Aurora was born because of you."

Her lips parted in surprise. "Because of me?"

He nodded. "I've read your journals, the poems, the stories. You wrote them for yourself, I know. You never wanted anyone else to see them. But when I read them, I understood. You don't just write words, Nisha. You capture truths people don't know how to say. That's what gave me the idea. If your words can do that, then there must be countless others out there waiting for the chance to speak."

A flush of heat rose to her cheeks, though her eyes quickly lowered. She remembered the sting of vulnerability when he'd first admitted to reading her hidden poems.

What he saw were only fragments, not the darker truths she now buried in a new journal, locked away where even he could not reach.

"I'll manage it," she said finally, her voice firm. "But I'll do it in my own way. If I'm to prove myself, I need freedom."

For a moment, Vijay studied her, his sharp gaze unreadable. Then, slowly, he nodded. "I trust you."

Lisa, who had been observing quietly, gave a small approving smile. The torch had been passed, not with ceremony, but with conviction.

From the next morning, Aurora Publishing House awakened like a hive stirring after long dormancy.

Staff who had worked under Edward Blackwood arrived with unease etched across their faces. Some carried resentment, others quiet hope. Rumors had spread about the Chandels' takeover, about the daughter now leading the house. To some, she was a mystery; to others, a risk.

But Nisha faced them directly. At the first general meeting, she stood at the head of the long conference room table, her voice calm and controlled.

"We are not here to erase your past," she said, her gaze steady as it swept across the room. "We are here to build a future. Aurora will not operate as Blackwood did. We will not favor only the famous, nor ignore the unknown. Every writer will be heard here, every story considered on its merit, not its name."

A murmur rippled through the staff. Some looked skeptical, but others straightened in their seats. Her tone was not fiery, but it carried weight, the kind that came from clarity.

Over the weeks that followed, change became tangible. The sterile boardroom walls were replaced with open discussion spaces. The editorial board was restructured, bringing in fresh talent alongside veterans. Acquisitions were reviewed with new eyes, focusing on emerging voices rather than only established bestsellers. Contracts were rewritten with fairer royalty splits.

And at the heart of it all, the "Aurora Masterclass Program" began to take shape.

Invitations were extended to renowned authors across London and beyond, poets, novelists, essayists, some wary, others curious. What publishing house offered mentorship? Yet the reputation of Chandel Enterprises carried weight, and slowly, names of significance agreed.

The day of the first masterclass arrived. Young writers filed into the freshly renovated auditorium; notebooks clutched like lifelines. Some wore nervous smiles; others carried the heavy silence of people who had never been taken seriously.

Nisha stood at the doorway, welcoming each one. Her face betrayed no nerves, but inside, her heart was tight with anticipation. These weren't just attendees. They were the voices Aurora had been built for.

When the session began, an established novelist spoke of failure, of manuscripts rejected dozens of times before success. The young writers listened, eyes wide, scribbling furiously. Later, one trembling student read her own short piece aloud, her voice breaking at first, then strengthening as the room fell into hushed silence.

Applause broke out. Tears shimmered in the girl's eyes.

From the back row, Vijay watched quietly. Lisa leaned toward him. "She's not just organizing. She's leading."

He smiled faintly. "Cold when she must be. Warm when she chooses to be. That balance… it's rare."

Nisha glanced toward them then, just for a second. She didn't smile, but her eyes gleamed with a fire neither of them had seen before.

Aurora was alive.

The rhythm of Aurora Publishing House settled into something vibrant, something alive. Each week, the masterclasses brought new faces, new voices, new revelations. The building, once burdened with the heavy silence of a dying press, now hummed with possibility.

One evening, the auditorium filled with a soft buzz of conversation. A celebrated poet had been invited to speak. He was old, his hair white, his voice carrying the gravel of years, but when he began to recite verses about love lost and found, the room grew still.

"Poetry," he said, pausing to look into the crowd, "is the language of wounds. You don't need to heal before you write. You write because you are wounded."

Those words seemed to ripple across the young audience. Some lowered their heads, hiding tears. Others clutched their notebooks tighter, as though they had just been given permission to bleed on paper.

Nisha, standing at the side, felt the words pierce her too deeply. Her face remained composed, but her chest tightened. She thought of her own hidden journal, the one she never let anyone touch. She thought of the nights when she wrote not for craft, not for beauty, but simply to survive her own silence.

After the session ended, a group of young writers lingered near the stage. One boy of barely twenty approached Nisha timidly.

"Ma'am," he said, fumbling with his notebook. "They never believed me at home. They said writing was useless, that I should find a real job. But here… for the first time, I felt like maybe it isn't foolish. Thank you."

She looked at him, her expression softening. "It isn't foolish," she said quietly. "It's a voice. And a voice is never useless."

The boy's eyes shone, and he bowed his head before leaving.

Lisa, who had been watching from the corner, gave a rare, approving nod. "He'll never forget those words," she murmured.

Nisha said nothing. She only pressed her notebook tighter against her side, as though guarding her own truths.

That night, long after everyone left, she remained behind in her office. London glittered beyond the windows, the Thames dark and restless. The building was silent, save for the faint hum of machines left on standby.

She unlocked the drawer and pulled out her hidden journal, the one her father didn't know about.

Her pen trembled at first, then steadied.

On a fresh page, she wrote:

"They think I am strong,

but strength is only the mask I stitched

from all the broken promises.

Do not touch it—

it may tear,

and beneath it, I am only bruises."

She read the lines back to herself, her chest tightening as if the words had unlatched a hidden wound. She turned the page quickly and began again, needing to disguise the rawness with the form of a story.

It was about a girl, nameless, faceless, who stood every evening by the river, waiting. Waiting for someone who promised to return.

"The city lights blurred into the water, but she could not see them. She only saw the reflection of what she waited for. They told her to move on, to forget, but the body does not forget. It carries memory like blood, like breath. She smiled to the world, but the river knew her silence."

Her eyes burned. She pressed the pen harder, forcing the words out.

"Coldness, they called it.

Cruelty, some said.

But if they knew how heavy love can become
when it has nowhere to go,

they would understand why she turned to ice."

The ink smudged under a tear that slipped onto the page. She didn't bother wiping it. This story was not for publication. Not for Aurora. Not for anyone. It was hers alone, the one wound she could never show her father.

For if he read this, she feared he would see her too clearly. And if he saw her pain, he would carry it as his own. She could not allow that.

She closed the journal abruptly at the sound of a knock on the door. Her heart lurched.

"Come in," she said, her voice steady though her hands trembled slightly.

It was Lisa, holding a folder. She looked at Nisha with her usual calm. "I thought you'd still be here."

Nisha forced a small smile, sliding the journal beneath a stack of papers. "Just finishing up."

Lisa set the folder on her desk. "Tomorrow's schedule. Another masterclass in the afternoon. And… your father wanted me to remind you of the board meeting."

"Thank you," Nisha said, her voice neutral.

Lisa lingered for a moment, her sharp eyes resting on Nisha's face as if she could see beyond the mask. But she said nothing, only nodded and left.

When the door shut again, Nisha leaned back in her chair, exhaling. Her secret was safe, for now.

Days turned into weeks, and Aurora bloomed. Stories poured in, manuscripts from unknown corners of the country, voices trembling but unyielding. The editorial board debated passionately, young interns ran through hallways carrying drafts. The once-forgotten building now pulsed with energy.

But each night, when silence returned, Nisha wrote.

"You cannot bury love," she scribbled one night, *"because love is not a body. It is air. You try to suffocate*

it, but it still seeps in through every crack, every breath. That is why forgetting is impossible. That is why silence hurts."

Another night, she wrote:

"He will never know

how many times I waited in the crowd,

how many times I almost called his name,

how many times I swallowed the words.

Love is cruel in silence,

but louder when denied."

The journal grew heavier with each entry, a mirror of her heart she dared not reveal.

And yet, the more she wrote, the stronger Aurora grew. The more voices she encouraged, the more she found herself secretly unraveling in her own.

Vijay sometimes walked in the corridors, unseen, observing. He noticed the writers flocking to her, the respect she commanded, the way she balanced firmness with compassion. He also noticed the exhaustion in her eyes, the way she lingered in her office long after everyone else had gone.

One evening, he paused by her door but didn't knock. Instead, he whispered to himself, "She carries more than I ever did at her age. But she must not break."

Inside, Nisha wrote on, pouring herself into the pages that no one would ever read.

Aurora was alive to the world. But in the shadows, another voice, her truest one, remained hidden, waiting.

***

Chapter 16
The Question

The night at Chandel Estate was quiet, except for the faint rustle of leaves stirred by the river breeze. The estate, grand yet timeless, seemed to hold its own silence, as though listening to the whispers within its walls.

In her room, Nisha sat at her desk, the journal open in front of her. Her eyes moved over the lines she had written earlier, words born of longing and fear.

"What if no one understands?

What if love is nothing but a wound

that keeps reopening each time I write?

What if silence is safer than truth?"

She stared at the ink until the letters blurred. For all her confidence at Aurora, for all the strength she showed the world, here she was just a girl burdened with doubts.

Her fingers brushed over the cover of the journal, then retreated. The words inside felt too heavy, too raw, too dangerous even for her father's eyes. Yet the confusion burned so strongly tonight that she could not keep it to herself.

Her gaze shifted to the faint light spilling from under the door of her father's study down the hall. She hesitated, then rose and wrapped her shawl around her shoulders. The decision came not with courage, but with desperation. She needed answers, maybe not all of them, but enough to quiet the storm inside her.

Vijay's study smelled faintly of paper and ink. Shelves of books lined the walls, some so worn that their spines bent with memory. A lamp burned steadily on his desk, casting a pool of golden light over scattered documents. But Vijay was not reading them. He sat with his eyes turned to the window, as if searching the night sky for something it refused to give.

When Nisha stepped inside, Vijay turned his head, and for a moment his sharp features softened.

"Nisha," he said quietly. "You're still awake."

"I couldn't sleep," she admitted, closing the door behind her.

He gestured toward the armchair opposite him. "Come, sit."

She obeyed, folding her hands tightly in her lap. For a while, neither spoke, and the ticking of the clock filled the room with measured silence.

Finally, Nisha looked up, her voice softer than usual. "Dad... can I ask you something personal?"

Vijay leaned forward, resting his elbows on the desk. "You can always ask."

She hesitated, then said, "How do you know if what you write is worth being read? How do you know if it's strong enough, or if it's just... weakness on paper?"

A faint smile touched his lips, though his eyes were serious. "Ah. So the journals continue."

She flushed, lowering her gaze. "It's nothing. Just... stories. I don't know why I even write them. Sometimes it feels pointless."

Vijay studied her carefully, then rose and moved to the window. He stood with his hands clasped behind his back, the city lights reflecting faintly in his eyes.

"Do you know what words are, Nisha?" he asked after a pause.

She frowned. "Words?"

"They are fragments of what we cannot say aloud," he said, his voice steady, deliberate. "People think writing is about being clever or polished. But the truth is simpler: we write because silence would destroy us. Writing is not weakness, it is survival."

Her lips parted slightly, his words cutting deeper than she expected.

"But what if people don't understand?" she whispered. "What if they reject it? Reject me?"

At that, Vijay turned. His gaze was intense, almost too heavy to hold. "Rejection," he said slowly, "is not the end of a voice. It is the test of it. Even the strongest words are turned away at first. What matters is whether you still dare to write after. That is when you discover your worth."

Something flickered in his expression then, something that hinted at memory. For a moment, his face carried a shadow she couldn't name.

"You speak like you've known it," she said carefully.

He gave a small, almost imperceptible smile. "Perhaps I have. Perhaps more than once. There are parts of me you do not yet know, Nisha. And maybe one day, when the time is right, you will understand."

The way he said it made her chest tighten. He wasn't lying. His words were not theoretical; they carried the weight of lived pain. But he spoke in riddles, never naming it.

"Why won't you tell me directly?" she asked quietly.

"Because," he replied, lowering his gaze to the desk, "some truths come only when we are ready to bear them. And some stories... they are understood better when life has given us the right eyes to see."

Nisha fell silent. Her heart ached with curiosity, but she knew pressing him would only close the door tighter.

At last, he walked back to his desk and placed his hand gently over hers. "Listen to me, Nisha. Don't hide your voice because of fear. Don't bury your words because of doubt. If they come from truth, they will find a place in this world. Even if it takes time. Even if it hurts."

Her throat tightened. "And if I fail?"

His gaze softened, though a quiet sadness lingered in it. "Then you will rise again. That is the only way. Failure does not break a voice; it tests whether it deserves to last."

For a long moment, she stared at him, seeing not just her father but a man carrying unspoken scars.

"Thank you, Dad," she whispered, fighting the sting in her eyes.

They sat together in silence, the clock ticking, the city breathing beyond the glass. Nothing more was said, but everything lingered: his cryptic words, his unseen pain, the sense that his story waited in the shadows.

When Nisha returned to her room, she opened her journal again. Her hand shook slightly, but this time her pen moved with more certainty.

"Maybe rejection will come,

but rejection is not silence.

It is proof I dared to speak.

And if I am broken,

then let me be broken loudly,

with words instead of silence."

She closed the book gently, pressing her hand to its cover. Somewhere deep inside, she understood: her father's encouragement carried the echo of his own past. And one day, when life demanded it, she would learn the story hidden behind his eyes.

But tonight, she had enough. Tonight, she had his faith.

Back in his study, Vijay remained seated long after the door had closed. The silence pressed against him, heavy and familiar. Slowly, his hand reached for the bottom drawer of his desk. From beneath stacks of reports and official files, he pulled out an old leather-bound journal. Its spine was softened from years of being opened and closed in solitude.

He flipped to a page at random, his eyes tracing words he had written in another time:

"London is bright tonight, but inside me it feels dim. The city moves forward, but I remain still. I finish meetings, sign contracts, speak to people who expect confidence from me. And yet when the day ends, I return

to silence. I eat alone. I walk alone. I sleep with thoughts that don't leave me."

His fingers lingered on the next line.

"They say love gives strength. Perhaps that's true, but one-sided love... it only empties you, little by little. Every morning, I wake with her face in my mind. Every night I close my eyes to the same memory. She never knew how much of me she carried. Maybe she never cared. Still, I cannot stop."

Vijay exhaled slowly, closing the journal with care. The ache in those words had not faded with time, it had only grown quieter, buried beneath layers of discipline and empire-building.

He slid the book back in the drawer beneath the official files as if covering a wound. His gaze lifted briefly toward the door where Nisha had left. She wrote to survive her silence; he had once done the same. Two journals, two hearts speaking in secret.

Leaning back in his chair, he closed his eyes. A name rose to his lips, whispered into the empty study, a name the world had forgotten but he never had.

And then the room returned to stillness, as if nothing had been spoken at all.

***

Chapter 17
The Journal

The house was asleep, wrapped in silence. Only the faint ticking of the clock in the hallway kept time with the whisper of the river outside. Nisha walked slowly down the corridor, her bare feet brushing against the cool wooden floor. She had told herself she only wanted to thank her father again or maybe ask one more question. But deep inside, something else pulled her toward his study.

The door was ajar. She pushed it gently, the hinges creaking softly. The lamp was off, the room dim, but the desk stood like a quiet sentinel. Papers were neatly arranged, yet one drawer was slightly open.

She hesitated, then stepped closer. Inside, beneath a stack of official files, something caught her eye: a leather-bound journal. It wasn't properly hidden, just slid under the documents as though placed there in haste. The corner of the cover stuck out enough for her to notice.

Her heart raced. She knew this was private. She knew she should turn away. But something inside her whispered that the answers she had been searching for were here, in these pages.

Slowly, she slid the files aside and pulled out the journal. The leather felt cool, rough, alive in her hands. Its edges were worn, its spine softened with time, the kind of book that had been touched many nights by the same pair of hands.

She opened it with trembling fingers.

The first entry read:

"First week in London. The city is loud, but I am quiet. I wake early, attend meetings, and push through the hours. I tell myself I am moving forward, but every step feels empty. I left everything behind, but her absence did not stay there; it followed me here. I thought a new place would mean a new heart. I was wrong."

Nisha's throat tightened. She turned the page.

"The office is filled with people, yet I have never felt lonelier. They look at me and see confidence, success, ambition. They do not see that at night, I return to an empty room. I cook for one, I speak to no one. My thoughts are full of her. Does she ever think of me? Or was I forgotten the day I left?"

Her hand trembled as she held the book closer. She could almost see her father, much younger, walking through unfamiliar streets with this pain lodged inside him.

She read on.

"They say time heals. But days are not healing me; they are sharpening the wound. Each morning, I open my eyes with her face in my mind. I go through routines, smile when expected, but the silence always wins when the night comes. I try to hate her for not seeing me, for never loving me, but I cannot. Love has made me weak, and I cannot even hate the one who gave me nothing."

Tears blurred Nisha's vision. She wiped them quickly, but they kept returning.

She turned to another entry.

"Success feels like dust. Today the company signed its first deal in London. They congratulated me, they raised glasses. I smiled, I thanked them. Then I came home, removed the tie, sat in silence, and wondered what the worth of it all was. What is the value of achievement if the one you love will never care? If every step forward feels like a step away from her?"

Nisha pressed her fingers against the page, as if she could ease the ache written there. Her chest ached with guilt. She had thought her pain was sharp, unbearable. But here was her father's suffering—endless, hidden beneath years of strength.

Another entry, written in hurried strokes, caught her eyes:

"Some nights I dream of speaking the words I never said. In the dream, she listens, her eyes soften, she understands. But I wake up and remembered she was never mine to begin with. Love without return is not love lived; it is love buried alive. And I bury it every morning, only for it to rise again by night."

Nisha covered her mouth with her hand, a sob threatening to escape.

The final entry she read that night was shorter, almost broken:

"I wonder if she ever knew how much of me she carried. Perhaps I was invisible. Perhaps my love was too quiet to reach her. But it was everything I had. And even now, though the world believes I am strong, I remain that invisible man, carrying a love that never belonged to me."

The journal slipped slightly in her hands as tears spilled freely down her face. She leaned back in the chair, holding the leather cover against her chest, her heart shattering with every line she had read.

For a long while, she just sat there, the silence of the study pressing in on her, broken only by the uneven sound of her breathing. It was as though the words of the past had carved themselves into her skin, each sentence carrying the weight of a father she thought she knew but had never truly seen.

Her father, the man who appeared so strong, so untouchable in front of the world, had once been as broken as she was now. His loneliness had stretched across oceans and years, written in ink that was never meant for anyone else to see.

Nisha pressed her forehead against the cool leather of the journal. *Was his pain the same as mine? Or was it heavier? Did he endure more than I ever could?* The thought twisted inside her, deepening the ache in her chest.

At last, with trembling care, she lowered the journal onto the desk. Her hands lingered on its cover, reluctant to let go, as though returning it meant burying his truth once again. Slowly, she slid it back into the drawer, beneath the stack of official files. She arranged the papers exactly as they had been, hiding the journal in the same careless secrecy her father had left it. With a soft push, the drawer clicked shut.

The study looked as though nothing had been touched. But Nisha knew everything had changed.

She rose quietly, legs unsteady, and left the room. The hall was darker now, the shadows longer. She moved back toward her room, each step heavier than the last.

Inside, she closed the door softly behind her and sank into her bed. The night wrapped around her, but it gave no comfort. Her eyes were swollen, her chest ached with the storm of emotions.

I thought I was alone in this pain, she whispered inwardly. *But he... he has lived with it longer than I have even breathed adulthood. And he never let it show. How did he carry so much for so long?*

The questions gnawed at her, sharp and endless. She pulled her knees to her chest and rested her chin on them, staring blankly into the dark.

She remembered his smiles at the dinner table, his calm tone in meetings, the way he motivated her with steady words. And now, behind all of it, she saw something else, the silence of a man who had once cried the way she cried now, but alone, without anyone to hold him.

Her tears returned, this time not just for herself but for him. They slipped down her face, soaking into her pillow when she finally lay down.

The journal's words echoed in her mind, relentless: *"Love without return is not love lived, it is love buried alive."*

Her heart was clenched. She thought of her own heartbreak, the wounds still raw. Was she burying her love too, just as he had? Was her story destined to mirror his?

Sleep did not come quickly. She lay awake for hours, her body tired but her mind restless. Between quiet sobs and ache of discovery, one thought lingered, haunting and unshakable:

Maybe he and I are more alike than I ever knew. Maybe we are both living with broken hearts the world will never see.

And with that, her eyes finally closed, damp with tears, as the house remained silent, guarding the secrets of father and daughter, two souls bound by pain neither had ever spoken aloud.

***

Chapter 18
Shadows of a Name

The morning light touched her room gently, but Nisha did not feel its warmth. Her eyes were still swollen from the night before. Sleep had come late, and when it did, it was restless, filled with her father's words scrawled in faded ink. Every line of that leather journal echoed in her mind, pulling her deeper into a silence she didn't know how to carry.

She tried to steady herself with routine, brushing her hair, pouring coffee, opening her laptop, but none of it held. The weight of what she had discovered pressed down heavier with each passing hour. She needed to speak to someone—someone who knew her father better than anyone else.

By noon, she found herself standing outside Lisa's cabin. The glass door was half-open; a stack of files balanced neatly on the desk inside. Lisa looked up from her work, adjusting her glasses.

"Nisha?" she said, her tone both surprised and warm. "You rarely come here unannounced. Is everything alright?"

Nisha stepped inside and closed the door behind her. For a moment, she didn't speak, her fingers twisting together nervously. "Lisa... you've been working with my father for a long time, haven't you?"

Lisa studied her carefully. "Yes. From the very beginning, when he first came to London to build all of this. Why?"

Nisha hesitated, then asked the question that had been pressing against her chest all morning. "Do you know anything about his past? Before the companies, before all this success... was there ever something... or someone he cared about deeply?"

The silence that followed was heavy. Lisa's eyes flickered, and she leaned back in her chair. She motioned for Nisha to sit. When Nisha did, Lisa folded her hands together on the desk and spoke quietly.

"You must never speak about this to anyone," Lisa said, her voice firm but gentle. "Your father has never shared that part of his life, not with the world, not with his colleagues, not even with me. And you are his daughter, Nisha. Sometimes it's better not to question what someone has chosen to bury."

Nisha's throat tightened. "But you've been with him for so long. You must have seen something. Some sign."

Lisa's eyes softened, a faint sadness crossing them. For a long moment, she didn't answer. Then she exhaled. "There's something you don't know, Nisha. When your father and I began building the company, I admired him more than anyone I had ever met. He was disciplined, brilliant, and determined. And somewhere along the way, I began to... care for him. More than I should have."

Nisha blinked, surprised. Lisa gave a faint, wistful smile.

"One evening, after months of working side by side, I gathered the courage to tell him. I told him I admired him, that I... loved him. He listened quietly, then refused just as quietly. He didn't embarrass me, didn't hurt me, but there was a wall there. A wall I could never cross. That was the day I understood, his heart already belonged to someone else, someone I would never meet."

Nisha's chest tightened. Her voice trembled when she spoke. "Last night... I read his journal. It was in his study. He wrote about a girl, again and again, but never her name. Do you... do you know who she was?"

For the first time, Lisa looked shaken. She turned her gaze to the window as though weighing whether to speak. Finally, she whispered, "Her name... was Venus."

The word seemed to linger in the air, heavy and unfamiliar, yet carrying an ache that Nisha felt in her bones. She repeated it softly, as though tasting it for the first time. "Venus..."

Lisa nodded. "I never met her. He never spoke about her in detail. But in those rare, unguarded moments, when his eyes drifted and his silence grew too long, I could tell she was still there in his thoughts. He admired her laughter; he once told me it sounded like winter bells. He said she had a kindness in her that could make anyone feel seen. And... he said she never belonged to him."

Nisha's heart ached. She remembered the entries in the journal, pages filled with longing, emptiness, and silence. Now the name gave them a face, a shape, even if still incomplete.

"Do you know what happened between them?" Nisha asked, her voice fragile.

Lisa shook her head. "No. He never let anyone close enough to know. All I can say is that whoever she was, she changed him. She made him who he is today, the man who built all this, the man who hides pain behind discipline. Even I, working beside him all these years, never broke through that silence."

Nisha lowered her gaze, her hands trembling in her lap. She whispered, almost to herself, "He's carried her all these years... and I never knew."

Lisa reached across the desk, placing her hand gently over Nisha's. "Sometimes, the strongest people are the ones who carry their scars in silence. Your father is one of them. But remember, Nisha, his silence was not because of you. It was because of her."

Nisha swallowed hard, tears burning her eyes. She pulled her hand back gently, nodding. "Thank you, Lisa."

She rose to leave, but her steps were slow, heavy. As she walked down the corridor, the name echoed in her mind, growing heavier with each repetition.

Venus. Venus. Venus...

The woman her father had loved, the woman he had never let go.

When she reached her room, Nisha closed the door and leaned against it, pressing her forehead to the wood. Her tears came quietly this time, sliding down her cheeks without resistance. She whispered into the silence, as though the walls could carry her question back to him:

Was my pain ever as deep as yours, Dad? Or was yours so much greater that mine will never compare?

She lay on her bed, staring at the ceiling, her chest hollow and full at once. The journal had given her his wounds. Lisa had given her a name. But the story itself remained hidden, suspended in shadows.

And that, perhaps, was the cruelest truth of all: that sometimes knowing just enough to hurt still leaves you with more questions than answers.

***

Chapter 19
The Price of Secrets

The late evening sun hung over London like a fading ember. Inside Chandel Enterprises, Vijay's cabin was shut tight, blinds drawn to half-shadow the room. A single photograph lay on his desk, the jagged outline of an island, dark against the restless sea.

Lisa entered, her tone respectful. "Sir, your guest is here."

"Bring him," Vijay said.

The door opened. A tall man walked in, his face expressionless, a thin folder tucked under his arm. His steps were steady, his presence quiet. To anyone else, he was just another contact. To Vijay, he was the shadow he had hired to chase what others wanted buried.

He set the folder on the desk and, with unhurried hands, drew out a photograph.

"The island," he said softly.

Vijay studied it, his jaw tense. "Tell me."

The man leaned forward, unfolding papers one by one. "It does not exist in records. No ownership, no registry. On paper, it's nothing. But I traced money, small transfers, fractured deliberately, routed through Cyprus, Malta, and the Caymans. They all loop back to one entity. A holding group without a name, hidden offshore. Whoever runs this has made sure no thread connects to them directly."

He slid another page forward, numbers scrawled, maps marked.

"There are vessels," he continued, his voice calm. "Unmarked. No flags, no identifiers. They dock at the island under cover of night. Cargo goes in, but not out. At least three shipments left London docks in the past two years and never reached their declared destinations. The trail ends near these waters."

Vijay's brows furrowed. "What kind of cargo?"

The man's lips pressed into a thin line. "Mixed. Official manifests say textiles, machinery, and medical supplies. But the numbers don't match. My sources whisper of weapons. Others say human cargo." He paused, his voice dropping lower. "Whatever it is, Mr. Chandel, people who ask too many questions vanish."

A silence thickened between them.

"And the locals?" Vijay asked finally.

"They won't speak of it," the man replied. "Fishermen avoid those waters. Those who once worked with the island's handlers have disappeared. The few who remain call it cursed. Not superstition—fear. Something happens there. Something worse than trade."

Vijay leaned back slowly, eyes locked on the photograph. "And the man?"

The detective produced another sheet with partial names and coded accounts. "Connected. Not directly, but through layers. Always through layers. He is linked, Mr. Chandel. The island and him... the same shadow."

Vijay's hand stilled against the desk. His voice, when it came, was steady, measured. "You are saying if I set foot on that island, I may not return."

The man gave a single nod. "That is exactly what I am saying."

Only the hum of the air conditioner filled the silence. Vijay stared at the image, a black shape rising from the sea, indifferent, unyielding. Then he said, calm but certain, "Make the arrangements. Quietly. I will go."

The man's gaze flickered once, but he gave no argument. He gathered the papers, leaving the photograph behind, and disappeared as quietly as he had entered.

Vijay remained at his desk, the island's shadow heavy in his thoughts.

That same night, at Chandel Estate, Nisha wandered through her father's study. The echoes of the name "Venus" haunted her still. The first journal she had found had left her shaken, but questions only multiplied. There had to be more.

She began to search.

She checked drawers carefully, files stacked neatly, contracts bound tight. Nothing. She moved to the bookshelves, running her fingers across leather spines, tilting them forward. One by one. Still nothing.

Her eyes caught a locked cabinet. She bent, pulling at the handle. It wasn't locked, only stiff. She tugged harder, and it creaked open. Inside lay old files, boxes stacked unevenly, layers of dust gathering on their corners.

Her pulse quickened. She reached in, pulling one box forward. Inside it was buried beneath faded reports and envelopes, another journal. Leather-bound, its cover darker, its edges frayed as though it had been touched too often, then abandoned.

Her hands trembled as she lifted it out. She sat in her father's chair, the journal heavy in her lap. Slowly, she opened it.

Entry 1

"The world feels unchanged, yet nothing is. Laughter still fills the streets, but to me it sounds hollow. I search the faces of strangers, hoping to find her shadow. But every corner is empty. Absence makes more noise than presence ever did."

Nisha exhaled shakily. It was cryptic pain threaded in every word.

Entry 2

"Each day I wake expecting her footstep at the door. Each night I wait for a voice that does not come. Can life erase itself so cleanly? Or is it only me who refuses to accept what I already know?"

Her heart pounded. Was this about separation or loss?

Entry 3

"They look away when I ask. Their silence is an answer louder than words. I feel the truth pressing, waiting. Yet I refuse to speak it. If I do, it will be real. And I cannot—will not—let it be real."

Nisha wiped her eyes quickly, but the words blurred anyway.

Entry 4

"The word was spoken at last. Sudden. Unexpected. A breath gone, a life ended in an instant. I was not there. I did not see. I cannot accept what my eyes never witnessed. Yet every whisper, every gesture confirms it: she is gone."

Her breath came shallow, dread filling her chest. She turned to the final page with trembling hands.

Entry 5 – Final Entry

"Tonight I write not to remember, but because forgetting is impossible. She is gone. Dead. The word cuts deeper every time I write it, but it is the only truth I have.

I was in London building futures, while the only future I wanted was being buried in the earth. I did not hold her hand. I did not hear her last word. They tell me she left peacefully. But how can peace exist in a stolen life?

Her name was Venus. To others, a name. To me, she was warmth in winter, kindness in chaos, light in every place that had only known shadow. Now she is silence. Eternal, cruel.

I rise, I build, I conquer, but it is all dust. She will never see it. She will never know.

There will never be another. She was the first. She will be the last. And I remain alive, though I no longer know why."

The journal slipped in Nisha's trembling hands. Tears spilled, staining the paper, as though the ink itself mourned.

She closed it carefully, clutching the leather against her chest. After what felt like hours, she slid it back into the box, burying it beneath the same files, leaving it as she had found it.

Back in her room, she lay in darkness, her father's grief now her own. Her lips parted, whispering the name that had changed everything:

"Venus..."

The word lingered in the air, unanswered, like a ghost that refused to fade.

Back in his office, the photograph of the island lay on the desk like a challenge. Vijay's phone buzzed once. Then twice. He glanced at the screen and saw messages arriving from numbers he did not know—anonymous, blunt, and cold.

They came one after another, short lines that did not explain but threatened:

"Turn back now."

"This island is not for the living."

"If you step there, there's no way out."

"They do not forgive trespassers."

"Consider this your only warning."

"Last chance—leave it."

Vijay read them slowly, the words settling in his chest like a weight. No name. No signature. Nothing to trace. Just the clear, flat certainty of a threat.

He set the phone down and stared at his own reflection in the dark glass of the window. Outside, London went on with lights, movement, and ordinary life, but inside that room, the air had changed. The island in the photograph looked sharper now, its edges less like scenery and more like teeth.

For a long time, he said nothing. Then, almost to himself, he whispered, "So someone knows." He did not ask who, and he did not tremble. There was a slow, hardening calm about him, the calm of someone who has already decided that some truths are worth the danger.

He slid the photograph back into the folder, folded the warnings into the thin private file he kept for troublesome matters, and closed the drawer with a soft, decisive click. The danger had moved from the abstract to the personal. The warning had not changed his plan; it had only sharpened his resolve.

Outside, the night fell. Inside, a different kind of darkness gathered: the quiet knowledge that one step toward the island might be the last step anyone would ever see him take.

***

Chapter 20
The Sky Fell Silent

The morning air at Chandel Estate carried the crisp chill of London's early hours. Nisha stood near the window, a cup of tea in her hand, watching the mist rise over the garden. She heard the sound of her father's footsteps behind her before she turned.

Vijay entered the room dressed for travel, his demeanor calm, his suitcase trailing lightly by his side.

"You're leaving?" she asked, her brow furrowing.

He gave her a faint smile, one that carried warmth but also distance. "Yes, Nisha. Something urgent has come up. Just business. I'll be back in a few days."

Her eyes searched for his face. "Do you have to go now? You've hardly rested these past weeks."

"Work doesn't wait," he said softly, placing a hand on her shoulder. His touch lingered longer than usual, as though he wanted to say more, but chose not to. "Look after the company while I'm gone. And... look after yourself too."

There was something unusual in his tone, subtle, quiet, but it left her unsettled. Still, she nodded, not wanting to press him. "Come back soon, Dad."

"I will," he promised, though even as he said the words, his eyes carried a weight she could not name.

Hours later, Vijay's private jet lifted into the gray London sky. He sat by the window, his phone in hand, the hum of the engines steady around him.

He opened his gallery. The screen lit up with images—Venus. Smiling in winter light, her hair falling across her face, her eyes holding a softness that time could not erase. One photograph, then another, each one pulling him deeper into the ache of memory.

He leaned back, closing his eyes for a moment, the phone resting against his chest. In the stillness, he whispered her name, so quietly the sound was swallowed by the roar of the sky.

Venus.

Outside, clouds gathered thick and dark.

At Aurora Publishing, Nisha sat at the long conference table surrounded by eager faces. A group of new authors, their manuscripts spread out before them, spoke about dreams, ideas, and the hope of seeing their words in print. She listened intently, offering encouragement, her mind half-distracted by her father's departure, but her heart focused on the passion in the room.

It was in that moment, when she was jotting notes in the margin of one manuscript, that her phone buzzed. Lisa's name flashed on the screen.

She excused herself and answered. "Lisa? I'm in a meeting..."

"Nisha," Lisa's voice was sharp, urgent, trembling in a way Nisha had never heard before. "Switch on the television. Now."

Something in her tone made Nisha's stomach drop. She hurried to the small TV mounted on the wall of the conference room. The room fell silent as she switched it on.

The news channel's breaking banner screamed in red across the screen:

"PRIVATE JET CRASHES OVER THE NORTH SEA—NO SURVIVORS FOUND YET."

Her heart stopped.

The anchor's voice carried on, words blurring as her vision narrowed: "Among the passengers believed to be on board is renowned businessman Vijay Chandel, head of Chandel Enterprises..."

The pen slipped from her fingers. The manuscripts scattered as she stumbled back, her body trembling.

"No..." the word tore from her lips, raw and broken.

The authors in the room froze, their eyes wide with shock. Some murmured her father's name, others whispered prayers. But Nisha could not hear them.

Her knees weakened, and she gripped the edge of the table to steady herself. Her chest heaved as the words on the screen repeated, hammering into her: "*Crash... no survivors... no bodies found.*"

Lisa's voice still echoed faintly through the phone she hadn't realized she dropped: "Nisha... are you there? Nisha..."

But Nisha could not answer. Her vision blurred with tears as she collapsed into the nearest chair, her hand covering her mouth as sobs broke free.

Her father—the one who had stood before her that morning, promising to return—was now gone. Taken by the sky.

At Chandel Estate that night, silence wrapped the halls like a shroud. Nisha sat alone in her room, her face pale, her eyes swollen from endless tears. The house felt emptier than ever before, the walls echoing with absence.

She replayed their last conversation in her mind—his hand on her shoulder, his quiet promise, his eyes that had seemed almost… final. Why hadn't she stopped him? Why hadn't she asked more questions?

Clutching one of his journals against her chest, she whispered into the darkness, "You said you'd come back. You promised."

But there was no answer. Only the hollow quiet of a world that had shifted in a single day.

And somewhere across the city, on every television, every newspaper headline, the same words burned:

"Vijay Chandel—Missing, Presumed Dead."

The sky had fallen silent.

Outside Chandel Estate's iron gates, the world was anything but silent.

Dozens of reporters crowded the entrance, their cameras flashing, voices rising into the cold night. News vans lined the road, headlights cutting into the mist. Microphones thrust forward through the bars of the gate as questions rang out:

"Is it true the jet was his?"

"Has the family confirmed?"

"What happens to Chandel Enterprises now?"

Security guards stood firm, but their presence only drew more onlookers. The estate, once a haven of peace, had become a spectacle.

Inside, the phones rang endlessly, calls from business partners, politicians, journalists. Employees of Chandel Enterprises sent frantic messages, their grief spilling into words of disbelief. Some gathered outside the company's headquarters, holding candles, their faces pale with shock. Others sat at their desks staring blankly at screens, unable to process the headlines.

Nisha watched the chaos unfold through the tall windows of her room. Her body was still, her face wet with tears, but her heart throbbed with an ache too deep to name.

She had spent the day trapped between shock and denial, clinging to every small hope. No bodies had been found, perhaps he was alive. Perhaps he had survived. Perhaps, perhaps, perhaps. Each thought was crushed by the cruel clarity of the news anchors repeating the same line: *"Vijay Chandel—Missing, Presumed Dead."*

Lisa finally arrived at the estate, her face grave, her voice steady for Nisha, though her own eyes betrayed sorrow. "Nisha, you must rest," she urged gently. "Tomorrow will bring questions. You will need strength."

But Nisha shook her head. She clutched one of her father's journals against her chest like it was the last piece of him she could hold. "He said he'd come back," she whispered, her voice cracking. "He promised."

Lisa placed a hand on her shoulder, unable to find words. The promise of a father had shattered into silence, and no reassurance could mend it.

Through the window, the reporters' cameras flashed, the frenzy of the outside world hungering for a statement. But Nisha could not move, could not face them.

All she could do was sit in the quiet of her father's absence, her heart breaking with the unbearable truth that the world believed: Vijay Chandel—her father, her protector, her anchor—was gone.

And though the city pulsed and clamored outside, inside the estate the silence deepened heavily, suffocating, final.

The sky had fallen silent.

***

Chapter 21
The Letters in the Silence

The great halls of Chandel Estate still echoed with footsteps, voices, and condolences that felt more rehearsed than heartfelt. The chandeliers glowed softly, portraits of ancestors watched from the walls, and trays of untouched tea sat cooling on polished tables.

All day, the house had been crowded with ministers, business partners, and journalists. They spoke of losses and legacies, but their eyes searched for reassurance... reassurance that Chandel Enterprises would not collapse with Vijay's absence.

Nisha stood through it all, nodding, bowing slightly, her heart a stone that could neither cry nor rest. She wanted to scream, to drive them out, but instead she pressed her lips together and let them say their words. Lisa moved through the crowd, shielding her as much as possible, but even she could not stop the tide of visitors.

By late evening, silence fell. The last car left the gates. The chandeliers dimmed. The mansion, once full of empty voices, now felt like a tomb.

Nisha sat by the fireplace, staring at the dying embers. That's when Lisa entered quietly. In her hands were two envelopes, the paper aged on one, the seal fresher on the other. Both bore Vijay's handwriting.

"Nisha," Lisa whispered, her voice breaking, "these were for you. He gave me the first one... many years ago, when you were still a child. The second, just days ago, before his last journey."

Nisha's breath caught. Her fingers trembled as she took them. Without a word, she walked to her father's study.

The room smelled of his cologne and old books. His chair was still slightly turned, as if waiting for him to return. She sat at his desk, lit a single lamp, and broke the seal of the older letter.

The First Letter

"My dearest Nisha,

If you are reading this, then something has taken me away from you sooner than I wished. I pray this letter reaches you with Lisa's care, because she has been my witness in all things. She knows what I write is truth.

You are not my daughter by blood. I never gave you life, but you gave mine its meaning. On a freezing winter night, years ago, I found you. You were wrapped in a thin cloth, left alone on the streets of London, your cries muffled by the sound of traffic. I had nothing then. I was struggling, building, fighting to stand in this foreign land. Yet, when I saw you… something inside me knew. I could not walk away. That moment, destiny placed you in my arms, and I never let go.

Lisa was with me. She tried to stop me. She said I had no resources, no home to give. But I told her, love will find a way. And it did. From that night, you became mine. Not born of me but chosen by me. Not bound by blood, but by the bond of my heart.

You are my daughter, Nisha. In every way that matters, in every heartbeat, in every sacrifice, you are mine. Do not let the world tell you otherwise. Never doubt that you are loved more fiercely than blood could ever demand."

Nisha pressed her trembling fingers to her lips. Her tears fell freely, smudging the ink. The ground beneath her life had shifted. She was no longer who she thought she was, yet the depth of his love thundered louder than the truth of her birth.

She turned to Lisa, who had quietly entered. "Lisa... this... is it true? Were you there that night?"

Lisa's eyes glistened as she nodded. "Yes, child. I was there. I held you before he did. I told him it was madness, that he couldn't afford another mouth when he had nothing. But he only said one thing: *'She is mine.'* And that was enough. From that moment, you were Nisha Chandel."

Her sobs deepened, torn between betrayal and belonging. She pressed the letter to her chest as if her father himself had embraced her.

Her hands reached for the second envelope, fresher, heavier. She broke the seal with a pounding heart.

The Second Letter

"Nisha,

By now, you have questions. Perhaps you have already searched for answers in my journals. Do not think I did not know. I left them within your reach because I saw your pain. I saw the shadow of one-sided love you carried, the silent ache you never confessed to me. It reminded me of myself. I had once promised you: if your love says no, I will tell you my story. And I was too weak to say it aloud. So, I let you find it in those pages.

But the journals cannot tell you everything. They hold fragments, not the whole. To know the truth about Venus, about me, about why I lived as I did, you must meet someone who carries the other half of the story. His name is ***Rachit Khare,*** *an IAS officer now posted in Haridwar, Uttarakhand. We studied together. He knows me as no one else does. I have already written to him. When you go, he will not turn you away.*

Nisha, do not think I am angry with you for reading those journals. You are my daughter. Your curiosity is the same as mine. But be ready, the truth will demand courage. Courage to see me not as your father alone, but as a man who loved, who lost, and who lived with pain he never spoke of.

Never forget, family is not in the blood, but in the love that binds us. You are mine, beyond doubt, beyond death. You will always be my pride.

—Your Dad"

Nisha's tears blurred the words. She turned to Lisa, whispering, "Did you… tell him I asked about Venus?"

Lisa shook her head firmly. "No, child. I never said a word. But you forget, he was your father. He knew everything. He knew his enemies' moves before they made them. He knew the truth behind silence. He knew you. That's why he was who he was."

Nisha's lips trembled. She clutched both letters to her chest, her sobs shaking her frame. For the first time, she felt utterly lost, her identity shaken, her heart splintered between love and pain, her path pointing toward answers she wasn't sure she wanted.

That night, she lay in bed, the two letters beside her pillow. Her father's voice lingered in her ears, his handwriting burned into her eyes.

And through the tears, one thought rose above all: *"Haridwar... Rachit Khare... maybe there, I will finally know who my father truly was."*

***

Chapter 22
The Diary of Lost Love

The chill of London still lingered in the early morning air as Nisha stepped through the wide glass doors of Heathrow Airport. A small black suitcase rolled behind her, but her steps were heavy, as if she were carrying the weight of the Chandel Estate itself on her shoulders. The headlines of the past week still rang in her ears: *"Vijay Chandel's Private Jet Crashes, Bodies Missing."*

Every step felt unreal. Every announcement at the airport was like a voice calling her into a world that no longer had her father in it. She remembered Lisa's trembling hand as she placed two letters in hers. She remembered the shattering truth: that she was adopted, found on the streets of London, and that her father's love was bigger than blood. She remembered the second letter too, the name of a man in India, *Rachit Khare,* who would tell her everything she longed to know about Venus.

She walked through security in silence, boarded her flight, and found her seat in business class. The world outside the oval window was gray, the London rain drumming softly on the glass.

As the plane climbed into the clouds, Nisha opened her leather-bound journal. Her pen hovered over the blank page for a long moment before the words spilled out.

Nisha's Journal – Entry 1

"It has been days, yet the silence in Chandel Estate still echoes in me. The house feels hollow, its walls

too wide, too cold. Everyone came to speak of him—ministers, businessmen, journalists—but none of them knew him the way I did. They didn't see the man who held his coffee in the mornings like it was his anchor. They didn't hear him humming quietly when he thought no one was listening.

Now I am alone with letters, with journals, with secrets that feel too heavy to carry. He spoke of Venus. I read of Venus. And then I read she is gone. But why do I feel as if her shadow still lingers between his words?

Dad, I don't know what I will find in India. But I must go. Because my heart refuses to let your story remain unfinished."

The hours stretched long above the clouds. She closed her journal and leaned back, eyes heavy with tears. When the plane landed in Delhi, the warmth of India embraced her like a sudden storm. It was evening. She boarded a train bound for Haridwar, her father's words burning inside her: *"Rachit Khare will tell you everything."*

The train rattled through the darkening plains. Outside, she saw flickers of small villages, people gathered by fires, the golden lights of roadside stalls. Each mile carried her closer to the truth, but also further from the world she knew.

At Haridwar station, Rachit Khare was waiting. He was older, his hair lined with silver, but his eyes were sharp and kind. He folded his hands gently. "Nisha," he said softly. "Your father once told me, if his daughter ever comes searching, I must be ready. Today… that day has come."

She swallowed hard, nodding silently. Together they walked to his official residence. It was modest, filled with books and old photographs. The ticking of a clock was the only sound.

Rachit offered her tea, but she could not drink. "Tell me about him," she whispered.

Rachit smiled faintly, a sadness flickering behind his eyes. "Your father was a man of fire and silence. Ambitious, yes, but when it came to Venus... he was nothing but a boy again. He loved her more than his own life. And yet, he carried that love like a wound he never allowed to heal."

Nisha's eyes brimmed. "He never told me her story."

Rachit nodded slowly. "He left that task for me. And he left this." He rose from his chair, opened a wooden cabinet, and took out an old leather-bound diary. He placed it in her trembling hands. "This is the first and only diary he ever completed. He wrote it when he was going to propose to her... after five years of silence."

Nisha held it close, her tears spilling freely. "Thank you," she whispered.

Later that evening, she checked into Pilibhit House, a riverside heritage hotel. Her room overlooked the Ganga, its waters silver in the moonlight. She sat by the window, the diary on her lap, and finally opened it.

***

The Diary of a One-Sided Love

My Favorite Incomplete Wish

The Prologue

"For more than a year, I've held onto this diary. To be honest, I bought it just for you, hoping to fill it with every feeling I had. Maybe these pages won't be completely full, because some moments are too special for words. This diary will tell you everything about your smile, your moments of ignoring me, and even your anger, which I know is often because of me. Maybe I think too much, but if I write this in chapters, it's because some things are just too important. Everything has felt wonderful since I first saw you. This diary is for you alone, my ***'Chota Tom,'*** *from your* ***'Heightened Jerry.'*** *'"*

Nisha pressed her lips together, her tears falling onto the page. She imagined him as a young man, trembling, uncertain, holding his pen like it was his only friend.

She turned the page.

The Beginning

"You don't know how this all started, how you became my college crush. It's a short story, but it's the most important one to me. It began on an October day. I was waiting for friends when I saw you. The sun hit your face, and your sweet smile took my breath away. It didn't just steal my breath; it took hold of my heartbeat. I'll never forget that feeling. I did so many silly things just to find out your name and your course. I even skipped classes just to stand outside your classroom and get a glimpse of you. That's what you do for a first love. As

*they say, '**The world paused when I saw your face, like my heart already knew its place.**'*

The saddest part was the days when I couldn't see you. I would spend the nights hoping you wouldn't be absent the next day. Weekends and holidays felt like torment. Then, I heard you had a boyfriend. It broke my heart completely. I felt like I couldn't share my feelings with anyone, so I didn't. But I was happy because loving someone means wanting them to be happy, no matter what. My one-sided love didn't last long, but it was a great time."

Nisha closed her eyes, whispering, "Dad…" as though he might answer.

She turned to the next entry.

A Second Chance

"Loving someone you can't have is a difficult thing. You just wait, hoping they will come to you, but you only hear echoes that were never there. From the bottom of my heart, I just want you to be happy. I want you to feel loved and appreciated.

The universe has its secrets. It brought you into my life twice. The first time was in college, and the second was years later at the same office, in the same department, in the same city. Still, I gave up because I thought I wasn't good enough for you. I tried to stay away, but the universe had other plans. Our manager changed, and we started talking for the first time outside of work. I was scared to talk to you because I knew my feelings would get stronger, and I wouldn't be able to handle another heartbreak. I was looking for a partner for my whole life, not just a girlfriend, and seeing you made me realize that I wanted you to be my better half.

When you're around, I feel lost. My heart and mind tell me to tell you how I feel. I feel incomplete without you.

The more days we spend together, the more certain I become. I cannot live with this silence. My feelings have grown too large to hide behind polite smiles and casual words. I've bought a ring—simple, silver, a quiet circle of promise. It reminds me of you: understated, yet shining in a way that humbles everything else.

I have rehearsed the words countless times. Sometimes in front of the mirror, sometimes whispering them into the night: "Venus, you were my first love, my only love. Will you marry me?" Each time my voice breaks. But tomorrow, I will not let fear hold me. Tomorrow, I will give you this diary, every word, every tear, every piece of me written here. You will know all of me at last."

Her fingers trembled as she turned the page.

"Tonight, I cannot sleep. The moonlight falls across my desk as I write, and I feel as if even the stars are waiting to see what tomorrow brings. My heart races when I imagine your face as you read these words. Will your eyes soften with understanding, or will they turn away in discomfort? I cannot know. But I know this: love is not meant to rot in silence. It must be spoken, even if it dies the moment it leaves my lips.

Venus, tomorrow I will place this diary in your hands. It holds the years of silence, the years of longing, the years I spent building the courage I never had. Whatever happens after, at least I will finally be free of silence. At least you will know."

Nisha's tears fell freely now. The window blurred as her sobs broke softly in her chest. She turned to the last entry.

The End of the Diary

"I've written a lot, but I want you to know a few things. ***'I'm always gonna wait for you.'*** *You will be the last person I ever love. I promise there will be no one after you. You are my favorite incomplete wish, a chapter in my life I want to read again and again, and I hope it never ends. My heart is only yours.* ***'Some may smile, others may stay, but my heart beats only one name every day, and that is yours.'***

If you say no, I will believe we weren't meant to be in this world. Maybe in a parallel universe we are. If not, then I will wish to God that in my next life, even if I have no name, fame, or money, I will have you because you are everything to me. Before that, I want to say something. If we are meant to be together, our love will be like ***Shiva and Parvati****, a story that was completed in the end. If not, it will be like* ***Radha and Krishna****, a love that may not be together, but is still eternal.*

Now, take care of yourself, V. I'm saying this because if we are not meant to be, I want you to be happy. But if we are, don't worry, your ***'Heightened Jerry'*** *is here to take care of you. Thank you for giving me so many wonderful memories. I will never forget you. You are my first and last love, and after this, there will be no one.*

I love you.

Now I'll explain how it happened with the Gods and Goddesses, the final offering that you never understood. I hope one day you will understand it when I'm no longer going to be with you."

The Final Offering

"I know my heart has poured a lifetime onto these pages, but before you read the end, I must speak of a truth that transcends us both. My love for you, V, is not merely human; it is a prayer, an offering placed at the feet of the divine.

If we are destined to be together, if our souls are meant to unite in this life, then our story will be a testament to a love like that of Lord Shiva and Goddess Parvati, a love that, through unwavering devotion and cosmic will, finds its blessed and eternal completion. May our paths merge as theirs did, a sacred union written in the stars.

But if our destinies lead us on separate journeys, then I will accept this path with a love as pure as that of Radha for her Krishna. I will not mourn a love unfulfilled in this world, but instead, I will find solace in knowing that my devotion to you is a form of bhakti, *a surrender to a higher purpose. Your memory will be the flute's melody that echoes in the depths of my soul, a sacred sound that keeps me tethered to the divine. For just as Radha's love for Krishna is eternal, so too is mine for you, a love that needs no physical union to be complete.*

And so, this is my final prayer to you, my dear V. Whether our story ends as Shiva and Parvati, or continues eternally as Radha and Krishna, please know this: my heart, a humble temple, will always house your name. You are the first and the last love I will ever know, and after this, my devotion rests, waiting for you in this life or the next.

I love you, now and forever."

When she finished reading, Nisha's hands shook so badly that the diary nearly slipped from her fingers.

Tears blurred her sight, spilling down her cheeks in an endless stream.

She pressed the diary to her chest, whispering into the empty room, "Dad... you loved her so much. You gave her all of yourself."

But her voice broke as she turned back to the final pages. The unanswered question tore at her soul: *What happened afterwards? Did she accept you, or did she walk away?*

Nisha leaned back against the chair, her sobs echoing softly in the riverside night. The Ganga flowed quietly beyond her window, carrying away her cries like prayers into the dark.

The chapter closed not with answers, but with a hollow ache. She now knew how much her father had loved Venus. But the mystery of what came next only grew larger, consuming her heart with desperate longing to know the end of a love story left unfinished.

To be continued...

Acknowledgements

Writing *The Curse of Not Being Chosen* has been a journey through silence, longing, and the quiet corners of the human heart. This story would not exist without the people who stood beside me, some with loud encouragement, some with soft understanding, and some simply with their presence.

To everyone who has ever loved in silence,

who has ever held feelings too fragile to speak aloud

this book is stitched with pieces of your courage.

Thank you for inspiring the heart of this story.

To the readers who saw themselves in these characters,

who felt understood in their heartbreak,

and who allowed these pages to echo their unspoken emotions

your connection is the greatest gift a writer can receive.

To my closest circle, the ones who listened to my ideas at odd hours,

who held space for my creativity,

and who reminded me that even the quietest stories deserve to be told

thank you for believing in me long before I believed in myself.

To the silent moments, the unfinished conversations, the unreturned affections,

and the tender wounds that taught me how deeply a heart can feel

thank you for giving me the truth from which this story was born.

And finally,

to the person who unknowingly shaped the emotional core of this book

your absence taught me more about love

than your presence ever could.

Some people are not meant to stay,

but they leave behind chapters that writers cannot help but write.

Thank you, from the deepest part of me,

for being part of this journey

for reading, for feeling, and for allowing this story

to touch the part of you that remembers what it is to love quietly.

With all my gratitude,

Vaibhav Singh Chandel

About the Author

Vaibhav Singh Chandel is a writer who draws inspiration from the smallest details, whether from his own life or the lives of those around him, and turns them into gripping works of fiction and poignant memoirs. He completed his undergraduate studies at Galgotias University, Greater Noida, and is currently pursuing an MBA from the University of Essex, London.

With a diverse background in theatre acting, assistant directing, and other creative fields, Vaibhav eventually found his true calling in writing. His work strives to redefine the concept of love, not merely as possession, but as a form of selfless expression and sacrifice. Exploring themes such as love, passion, drama, business, and the intricate complexity of human relationships, his writing captures the bittersweet essence of life's journey.

His debut novel, *The Curse of Not Being Chosen*, is the first installment of a planned trilogy. It delves into themes of love, drama, resentment, and the transformative journey from nothing to everything.

Vaibhav can be contacted at: vaibhav.98chandel@gmail.com